"WE WERE NOT THIS SHIP'S DESTINATION," THE OLD MAN TOLD ROSS.

"We weren't even the first alternate—or the second alternate. To be exact, Ross, we were the seventh choice for this ship."

Ross let go of his stanchion, floated a yard, and flailed back to it. "That's ridiculous, Mr. Haarland," he protested.

Haarland said steadily, "It is conceivable, of course, that the first-choice planet somehow didn't pick the ship up when this longliner came into radar range. In that event, of course, it would orbit once or twice on automatics, and then select for its first alternate target—which it did." He nodded earnestly. "Once, Ross. Not six times. No planet passes up a trading ship. Six different planets, all listed on the traditional star charts as inhabited, civilized, equipped with GCA radars, and everything else needed—six planets which are now out of communication."

FREDERIK POHL AND C. M. KORNBLUTH
SEARCH THE SKY

BAEN
science fiction
BOOKS

SEARCH THE SKY

This is a work of fiction. All the characters and events portrayed in this book are fictional, and any resemblance to real people or incidents is purely coincidental.

A Baen Book

Baen Enterprises
260 Fifth Avenue
New York, N.Y. 10001

First printing, October 1985

ISBN: 0-671-55989-3

Cover art by Vincent DiFate

Printed in the United States of America

Distributed by
SIMON & SCHUSTER
MASS MERCHANDISE SALES COMPANY
1230 Avenue of the Americas
New York, N.Y. 10020

for Jim Patrick,
who gave us a second turn at bat.

1

Decay.

That was the word that kept bobbing to the surface of Ross's mind. The word decay. The very smell of decay. The alway-there, never-quieted sensation of decay that had been part of the furnishings of his head as far back as he could remember. As he stood on the trader's ramp, overlooking the bustling and very underdecayed Yards, he heard it sounding in his ear.

Decay.

The funny thing was that hardly anybody Ross knew could see it or smell it. If he said the word "decay" to his boss, or to one of his neighbors, or to the occasional girl he ventured a single and unsatisfying date with, they didn't seem to know how to grasp his point. They understood the word, all right. They just attached different meanings to it. "Decay" meant what happened when you didn't put your food scraps in the disposer after dinner, or what happened to one of the derelicts in Ghost

Town when he died and no one noticed for a week or two . . . or, rarely, what happened to your teeth if you didn't remember to check in with the auto-medics twice a standard year.

What it didn't mean to any of them was what it meant to Ross: the almost imperceptible reek of dead and rotting dreams and plans that hung over every square foot of Halsey's Planet. Well, not every square foot. There were exceptions. The clean, big, bustling spaceport called "the Yards" was one of them, but they just made the sensation stronger. From where he stood on the height of the ramp he could see the undecayed activity of the Yards, and the only slightly spoiled spires of Halsey City, ten kilometers away on its other side. . . .

And he could also see, between spaceport and city, the thoroughly decrepit tumble-down gray acres of Ghost Town. Ghost Town was the heart of the rot, and the rot was spreading.

Ross wrinkled his nose. He couldn't help it, though he had long ago become sure that the stench was in his mind rather than in his nostrils. It was the stink (he had been told, by one of those infrequent young women who accepted a date with an obvious loser) of his own brooding he smelled, and why didn't he just lighten up and go for the good things like everybody else? He had tried. God knew he had tried; but the smell kept coming back.

This morning it was worse than usual. It had saturated his nostrils since first he woke; it had spoiled his breakfast, although there was actual fresh fruit on the table, for a miracle. It was no doubt what had kept him tossing and turning all the weary night, though the other possible explanation was that he had been wrestling with the hardest decision of his life. Well, that was true enough. And he had made the decision; and he had got up early, so early that the only thing that made sense, after deciding not to try to swallow the breakfast he had picked at, was to walk to work.

Nobody walked to work at the Yards. It meant you had to walk through Ghost Town.

There wasn't anything really frightening about Ghost Town, though he hadn't walked through it in a long time—not since childhood, in fact. That was a whole other thing. It was like taking a dare to go inside a haunted house. For children, Ghost Town was a wonderful place to play. Tag, Follow My Fuehrer, Senators and President—all the old chase-and-catch games were even more fun in Ghost Town than in the bland and unworrying streets where normal people still lived. The games took on new exciting life when you played them where you were dodging and turning through the crumbling ruins that had once been ranch houses and fast-food franchises and supermarkets, where you darted down lanes whose street signs had moldered away for a generation or two since anyone last looked for an address there and galloped past sagging shacks which now and then—and heart-stoppingly—might erupt a screeching, unexpected hermit to hide from and taunt.

All that was true of Ghost Town. The other thing that was true of Ghost Town—Ross was sure of it, though it didn't come up much in polite conversation—was that just in the couple of decades since Ross himself was one of those adventuring kids, Ghost Town had grown a good deal larger.

Everybody knew that even if they didn't like to discuss it. Ask the right specialists, and they'd tell you how much and how fast Ghost Town had grown. An acre a year, a street a month, a block a week, the specialists would twinkle at you, convinced that the acre, street, block was under control, since they could measure it.

Ask the right specialists and they would tell you why it was happening. One answer per specialist, with an iron-clad guarantee that there would be no overlapping of replies. "A purely psychological phenomenon, Mr. Ross. A vibration of the pendulum toward greater municipal compactness, a huddling, a mature recognition of the facts of interdependence, basically a step forward. . ."

"A purely biological phenomenon, Mr. Ross. Falling birth rate due to biochemical deficiency of trace elements processed out of our planetary diet. Fortunately the situation has been recognized in time and my bill before the Chamber will provide . . ."

"A purely technological problem, Mr. Ross. Maintenance of a sprawling city is inevitably less efficient than that of a compact unit. Inevitably there has been a drift back to the central areas and the convenience of air-conditioned walkways, winterized plazas . . ."

Yes. It was a purely psychological-biological-technological-educational-demographic problem, and it was basically a step forward.

Ross wondered how many Ghost Towns lay corpselike on the surface of Halsey's Planet. Decay, he thought. Decay.

But it had nothing to do with the decision he had made, about the problem that had kept him awake all the night, the problem that blighted the view before him now.

The trading bell clanged. The day's work began.

For Ross it might be his last day's work at the Yards.

*   *   *

He walked slowly from the ramp to the offices of the Oldham Trading Corporation. "Morning, Ross boy," his breezy young boss greeted him. Charles Oldham IV's father had always taken a paternal attitude toward his help, and Charles Oldham IV was not going to change anything that Daddy had done. He shook Ross's hand at the door of the suite and apologized because they hadn't been able to find a new secretary for him yet. They'd been looking for two weeks, but the three applicants they had been able to dredge up had all been hopeless. "It's the damn Chamber," said Charles Oldham IV, winsomely gesturing with his hands to show how helpless men of affairs were against the blundering interference of Government. "Damn labor shortage is nothing but a damn artificial scarcity crisis. Daddy saw it; he knew it was coming."

Ross almost told him he had decided to quit, but held back. Maybe it was because he didn't want to spoil Oldham's day with bad news, right on top of the opening bell. Or maybe it was because, in spite of a sleepless night, he still wasn't quite sure.

The morning's work helped him to become sure. It was the same monotonous grind.

Three freighters had arrived at dawn from Halsey's third moon, but none of them was any affair of his. There was an export shipment of jewelry and watches to be attended to, but the ship was not to take off for another week. It scarcely classified as urgent. Ross worked on the manifests for a couple of hours, stared through his window for an hour, and then it was time for lunch.

Little Marconi hailed him as he passed through the traders' lounge.

Of all the juniors on the Exchange, Marconi was

the one Ross found easiest to take. He was lean and dark where Ross was solid and fair; worse, he stood four ranks above Ross in seniority. That was no small thing. Status was an important matter in the rigid (they called it "orderly") and fairly fossil-ized (they called it "tradition-respecting") social standards of Halsey's Planet. But Ross worked for Oldham and Marconi worked for Haarland's. They were not in the same hierarchical chain, and so the difference in position could be overlooked in social intercourse.

Social intercourse was what they had in com-mon. The other thing they had in common was their work which, for both of them, entailed months or years, even decades, of dull squeezing out of tiny margins of profit in the humdrum dealings between the cities of Halsey's Planet, and the only slightly more exciting commerce with the hayseed traders who occupied its moons—with the explosive sunburst of excitement every now and then when a longliner came in and all the traders swarmed into frenzied action. Compared with most careers on Halsey's Planet, they were dream jobs. Ross didn't find them so. He suspected that Marconi didn't either, and that was a link. The other thing that drew them together was that Marconi's read-ing, like Ross's, was not confined to bills of lading. Both of them were of exploring and curious turns of mind ... even about the subjects that were not generally mentioned in polite discourse—and which, of course, they had seldom discussed explicitly even between themselves.

The subject of decay, for example.

Nevertheless, Marconi was the closest thing to a friend Ross had. Marconi obviously shared the feel-ing. "Lunch?" he asked. "Sure," Ross said, and knew that it was very likely that he would spill his secret within the next hour to the little man from Haarland's.

The skyroom was crowded—comparatively—which meant that all eight of the tables that were normally used were already taken. They pushed on to the roped-off area by the windows and found a table that overlooked the Yards. It obviously had not been needed, or cleaned off, in many weeks. Marconi blew dust off his place setting with a humorous lift of the eyebrows and shrugged. "Care for a drink?" he asked, knowing what the answer would be, and looked astonished when Ross nodded firmly. It was not the way things usually went. Marconi was the one usually who had a drink with lunch, Ross never touched it.

When the drinks came, each of them said to the other in perfect synchronism: "I've got something to tell you."

They looked startled—then laughed. "Go ahead," said Ross.

The little man didn't even argue. Rapturously he drew a photo out of his pocket.

God, thought Ross wearily, Lurline again! He studied the picture with a show of interest. "New snap?" he asked brightly. "Lovely girl—" Then he noticed the inscription: *To my fiancé, with crates of love.* "Well!" he said, "Fiancé, is it now? Congratulations, Marconi!"

Marconi was almost drooling on the photo. "Next month," he said happily. "A big, big wedding. For keeps, Ross—for keeps. With children!"

Ross made an expression of polite surprise. "You don't say!" he said.

"It's all down in black and white! Lurline agrees to have two children in the first five years—no permissive clause, a straight guarantee. Fifteen hundred annual allowance per child. And, Ross, do you know what? Her lawyer told her right in front of me that she ought to ask for three thousand, and she told him, 'No, Mr. Turek. I happen to be in love.' How do you like that, Ross?"

"A girl in a million," Ross said feebly. His private thoughts were that Marconi had been gaffed and netted like a sugar perch. Lurline was a daughter of the Old Landowners, who didn't own anything much but land these days, and Marconi was an undersized nobody who happened to make a very good living. Sure she happened to be in love. Smartest thing she could be. Of course, promising to have children sounded pretty special; but the papers were full of those things every day. Marconi could reliably be counted on to hang himself. He would promise her breakfast in bed every third weekend, or the maid that he couldn't possibly find on the labor market, and so the courts would throw all the promises on both sides out of the contract as a matter of simple equity. But the marriage would stick, all right.

Marconi had himself a final moist, fatuous sigh and returned the photo to his pocket. "And now," he asked brightly, craning his neck for the waiter, "what's your news?"

Ross sipped his drink, staring out at the nuzzling freighters in their hemispherical slips. He said abruptly, "I might be on one of the moon ships next week. Fallon's got a purser's berth open."

Marconi forgot the waiter and gaped. "Quitting?"

"I've got to do something!" Ross exploded. His own voice scared him; there was a knife blade of hysteria in the sound of it. He gripped the edge of the table and forced himself to be calm and deliberate.

Marconi said tardily, "Easy, Ross."

"Easy! You've said it, Marconi: 'Easy.' Everything's so damned easy and so damned boring that I'm just about ready to blow! I've got to do something," he repeated. "I'm getting nowhere! I push papers around and then I push them back again. You know what happens next. You get soft and paunchy. You find yourself going by the book instead of by your head. You're covered, if you go by the book—no matter what happens. And you might just as well be dead!"

"Now, Ross——"

"Now, hell!" Ross flared. "Marconi, I swear I think there's something wrong with me! Look, take Ghost Town for instance. Ever wonder why nobody ever lives there, except a couple of crazy old hermits?"

"Why, it's Ghost Town," Marconi explained. "It's deserted."

"And why is it deserted? What happened to the people who used to live there?"

Marconi shook his head. "You need a vacation, son," he said sympathetically. "That was a long time ago. Hundreds of years, maybe."

"But where did the people go?" Ross persisted desperately. "All of the city was inhabited hundreds of years ago—the city was twice as big as it is now. How come?"

Marconi shrugged. "Dunno."

Ross collapsed. "Don't know. You don't know, I don't know, nobody knows. Only thing is, I care! I'm curious, Marconi. I get—well, moody. Depressed. I get to worrying about crazy things. Ghost Town, for one. And why can't they find a secretary for me? And am I really different from everybody else or do I just think so—and doesn't that mean that I'm insane?"

He laughed. Marconi said warmly, "Ross, you aren't the only one; don't ever think you are. I went through it myself. Found the answer, too. You wait, Ross."

He paused. Ross said suspiciously, "Yeah?"

Marconi tapped the breast pocket with the photo of Lurline. "The right one will come along," he said.

Ross managed not to sneer in his face. "No, she won't," he said wearily. "Look, I don't advertise it, but I was married once. I was eighteen, it lasted for a year and I'm the one who walked out. Flat-fee settlement; it took me five years to pay off the loan, but I never regretted it."

Marconi began gravely, "In the case of sexual incompatibility—"

Ross cut him off with an impatient gesture. "In that department," he said, "it so happens she was a genius. But—"

"But?"

Ross shrugged. "I must have been crazy," he said shortly. "I kept thinking that she was half-dead, dying on the vine like the rest of Halsey's Planet. And I must still be crazy, because I still think so."

The little man involuntarily felt his breast pocket. He said gently, "Maybe you've been working too hard."

"Too hard!" Ross laughed, a curious blend of true humor and self-disgust. "Well," he admitted, "I need a change, anyhow. I might as well sign on for a longliner. At least I'd have my spree to look back on."

"No!" Marconi said, so violently that Ross slopped the drink he was lifting to his mouth. He wasn't the only one startled by the unexpected explosion. On the other side of the ropes, diners at the regular tables glanced over, peevishly or curiously.

It took a moment for the buzz in the restaurant to establish itself again, and Ross spent it looking hard at the little man. He did what he had never done before. He signaled for another round of drinks, and then he said, "So all right, then, Marconi. It's no. But tell me something?"

Marconi gave him an opaque look. "Tell you what?"

"Tell me what I just said that blew your fuse. Was it the word longliner?"

"I don't know what you're talking about, Ross."

"You do, though. Tell me."

The little man licked his lips and his eyes roved around the restaurant worriedly. "I mean it, Marconi," said Ross.

"Well. . . . Well, hell, Ross! You know what a longliner is like! You go off in a damn old spacecraft, with gutter-scrapings for crew and very little hope that you'll live to reach your destination."

"No," Ross said, "actually I don't know. Hardly anybody seems to, except a couple people like you, and you won't talk about it. When I ask you what a longliner is, what the crew do with themselves for two or three centuries, you change the subject. You always change the subject! Maybe you know something I don't know. I want to know what it is, and this time the subject doesn't get changed. You don't get off the hook until I find out." He took a sip of his new drink and leaned back. "Tell me about longliners," he said. "I've never seen one coming

in; it's been fifteen years or so since that bucket
from Sirius IV, hasn't it? But you were on the job
then?"

Marconi was no longer a man in love or one of
the few people whom Ross considered to be wholly
alive—like him. He was a hard-eyed little stranger
with a stubborn mouth and an ingratiating ve-
neer. In short he was again a trader, and a good
one.

"I'll tell you anything I know," Marconi declared
positively, and insincerely. "Tend to that fellow
first though, will you?" He pointed to a uniformed
Yards messenger whose eye had just alighted on
Ross. The man threaded his way, stumbling, through
the tables and laid a sealed envelope down in the
puddle left by Ross's drink.

"Sorry, sir," he said crisply, wiped off the envelope with his handkerchief and, for lagniappe, wiped
the puddle off the table into Ross's lap.

Speechless, Ross signed for the envelope on a
red-tabbed slip marked URGENT * PRIORITY *
RUSH. The messenger saluted, almost putting his
own eye out, and left, crashing into tables and
chairs.

"And that's another thing," Ross muttered, following the man with his eyes.

"What's that?"

"Incompetence, Marconi! Stupidity. A general
and progressive loss of skills and talents that is
by-God real and that nobody by-God wants to talk
about."

Marconi didn't change expression, but his body-
language announced a slight relaxation with the
change of subject. "I don't know what that has to
do with the other business," he said. "Anyway,
why don't you just relax? You don't want to start

this stuff over again. I admit the guy is a jerk, but—"

"He's not just a jerk. He's halfway to just plain dead. I don't know why he bothers to stay alive at all. Don't try to tell me you don't know something's wrong, Marconi! He's a bumbling incompetent, and half his generation is just like him." He looked bitterly at the envelope and dropped it on the table again. "More manifests," he said. "I swear I'll start throwing tableware if I have to check another bill of lading. Brighten my day, Marconi; tell me about the longliners. You're not off the hook yet, you know."

Marconi signaled for a third round. "All right," he said. "Marconi tells all about longliners. They're ships. They go from the planet of one star to the planet of another star. It takes a long time, because stars are many light-years apart and rocket ships cannot travel as fast as light. Einstein said so—whoever Einstein was. Do we start with the Sirius IV ship? I was around when it came in, all right. Fifteen years ago, and Halsey's Planet is still enjoying the benefits of it. And so is Leverett and Sons Trading Corporation. They did fine on flowers from seeds that bucket brought, they did fine on sugar perch from eggs that bucket brought. I've never had it myself. Raw fish for dessert! But some people swear by it—at five shields a portion. They can have it."

"You're still on the hook, Marconi," Ross reminded grimly.

Trader Marconi laughed amiably. "Sorry. Well, what else? Pictures and music, but I'm not much on them. I do read, though, and as a reader I say, God bless that bucket from Sirius IV. We never had a novelist like Morris Halliday on this planet—

or an essayist like Jay Waring. Let's see, there have been eight Halliday novels off the microfilms so far, and I think Leverett still has a couple in the vaults. Leverett must be——"

"Marconi. I don't want to hear about Leverett and Sons. Or Morris Halliday, or Waring. I want to hear about longliners."

"I'm trying to tell you," Marconi said sullenly, the mask down.

"No, you're not. You're telling me that the longline ships go from one stellar system to another with merchandise. I know that."

"Then what do you want?"

"Don't be difficult, Marconi. I want to know the facts. All about longliners. The big hush-hush. The candid explanations that explain nothing—except that a starship is a starship. I know that they're closed-system, multigeneration jobs; a group of people get in on Sirius IV and their great-great-great-great-grandchildren come giggling and stumbling out on Halsey's Planet. I know that every couple of generations your firm—and mine, for that matter—builds one with profits that would be taxed off anyway and slings it out, stocked with seeds and film and sound tape and patent designs and manufacturing specifications for every new gimmick on the market, in the hope that it'll be back long after we're dead with a similar cargo to enrich your firm's and my firm's then-current owners. Sounds silly—but, as I say, it's tax money anyhow. I know that your firm and mine staff the ships with half a dozen bums of each sex, who are loaded aboard with a dandy case of delirium tremens, contracted from spending their bounty money the only way they know how. And that's just about all I know. Take it from there, Marconi. And be specific."

The little man shrugged irritably. "That gag's beginning to wear thin, Ross," he complained. "What do you want me to tell you—the number of welds in Bulkhead 47 of Starship 74? What's the difference? As you said, a starship is a starship is a longliner. Without them the inhabited solar systems would have no means of interstellar contact or commerce. What else is there to say?"

Ross looked suddenly lost. "I—don't know," he said. "Don't you know, Marconi?"

Marconi hesitated, and for a moment Ross was sure he did know—knew something, at any rate, something that might be an answer to the doubts and nagging inconsistencies that were bothering him. But then Marconi shrugged and looked at his watch and ordered another drink.

But there was something wrong. Ross felt himself in the position of a diagnostician whose patient willfully refuses to tell where it hurts. The planet was sick—but wouldn't admit it. Sick? Dying! Maybe he was on the wrong track entirely. Maybe the starships had nothing to do with it. Maybe there was nothing that Marconi knew that would fit a piece into the puzzle and make the answer come out all clear—but Ghost Town continued to grow acre by acre, year by year. And Oldham still hadn't found him a secretary capable of writing her own name.

"According to the historians, everything fits nicely into place," Ross said, dubiously. "They say we came here ourselves in longliners once, Marconi. Our ancestors under some man named Halsey colonized this place, fourteen hundred years ago. According to the longliners that come in from other stars, their ancestors colonized wherever they came from in starships from a place called Earth. Where is this Earth, Marconi?"

Marconi said succinctly, "Look in the star charts. It's there."

"Yes, but—"

"But, hell," Marconi said in annoyance. "What in the world has got into you, Ross? Earth is a planet like any other planet. The starship Halsey colonized in was a starship like any other starship— only bigger. I guess, that is—I wasn't there. After all, what are the longliners but colonists? They happen to be going to planets that are already inhabited, that's all. So a starship is nothing new or even very interesting, and this is beginning to bore me, and you ought to read your urgent-priority-rush message."

Ross felt repentant—knowing that that was just how Trader Marconi wanted him to feel. He said slowly, "I'm sorry if I'm being a nuisance, Marconi. You know how it is when you feel stale and restless. I know all the stories—but it's so damned hard to believe them. The famous colonizing ships. They must have been absolutely gigantic to take any reasonable number of people on a closed-circuit, multigeneration ride. We can't build them that big now!"

"No reason to."

"But we couldn't if we had to. Imagine shooting those things all over the Galaxy. How many inhabited planets in the charts—five hundred? A thousand? Think of the technology, Marconi. What became of it?"

"We don't need that sort of technology any more," Marconi explained. "That job is done. Now we concentrate on more important things. Learning to live with each other. Developing our own planet. Increasing our understanding of social factors and demographic——"

Ross was laughing at last. "Well, Marconi," he said at last, "that takes care of that! We sure have figured out how to handle the social factors, all right. Every year there are fewer of them to handle. Pretty soon we'll all be dead, and then the problem can be marked 'solved.'"

Marconi laughed too—eagerly, as if he'd been waiting for the chance. He said, "Now that that's settled, are you going to have some lunch?"

The Yards messenger stumbled up to their table again, this time with an envelope for Marconi. He looked sharply at Ross's unopened envelope and said nothing, pointedly. Ross guiltily picked it up and tore it open. You could act like a sulky child in front of a friend, but strangers didn't understand.

The message was from his office. RADAR REPORTS HIGH VELOCITY SPACECRAFT ON AUTOCONTROLS. FIRST APPROXIMATION TRAJECTORY INDICATES INTERSTELLAR ORIGIN. PROBABLE ETA YARDS 1500. NO RADIO MESSAGES RECEIVED. DON'T HAVE TO TELL YOU TO GET ON THIS IMMEDIATELY AND GIVE IT YOUR BEST. OLDHAM.

Ross looked at Marconi, whose expression was perturbed. "Bet I know what your message says," he offered with an uneasy quaver in his voice.

Marconi said: "I'll bet you do. Oldham's radar setup on Sunward always has been better than Haarland's. Better location. Man, you are in trouble! Let's get out there and hope nobody's missed you so far."

They grabbed sandwiches from the snack bar on the way out and munched them while the Yards jeep took them to the ready line. Skirting the freighters in their pits, slipping past the enormous

overhaul sheds, they saw excited debates going on.
Twice they were passed by Yards vehicles heading
toward the landing area. Halfway to the line they
heard the recall sirens warning everybody and everything out of the ten seared acres surrounded by
homing and Ground-Controlled Approach radars.
That was where the big ones were landed.

The ready line was jammed when they got there.
Ships from one or another of the five moons that
circled Halsey's planet were common; the moons
were the mines. Even the weekly liner and freighters from the colony on Sunward, the planet next
in from Halsey's, were routine to the Yards workers. But to anybody, an interstellar ship was a
sensation, a once-or-twice-in-a-lifetime thrill.

Protocols were uncertain. Traders argued about
who would get the first crack at the strangers and
their goods. A dealer named Aalborg said the only
fair system would be to give every trader there an
equal opportunity to do business—in alphabetical
order. Everybody else laughed him down. Everybody agreed that under no circumstances should
the man from Leverett and Sons be allowed to
trade—everybody, except the man from Leverett
and Sons. He pointed out that his firm was the
logical choice because it had more and fresher
experience in handling interstellar goods than any
other. . . .

They almost mobbed him.

It wasn't merely money that filled the atmosphere with electric tingles. The glamor of time-
travel was on them. The crew aboard that ship
were travelers of time as well as space. The crew
that had launched the ship was dust. The crew
that served it now had never seen a planet.

That was what being a longliner meant.

There was even some humility in the crowd. There were thoughtful ones among them who reflected that it was not, after all, a very great feat to hitch a rocket to a shell and lob it across a few million miles to a neighboring planet. It was eclipsed by the tremendous deed whose climax they were about to witness. The thoughtful ones shrugged and sighed as they thought that even the starship booming down toward Halsey's Planet—fitted with the cleverest air replenishers and the most miraculously efficient waste converters—was only a counter in the game whose great rule was the mass-energy formulation of the legendary Einstein: that there is no way to push a material object past the speed of light.

A report swept the field that left men reeling in its wake. Radar Track confirmed that the ship was of unfamiliar pattern. All hope that it might be a starship launched from this very spot on the last leg of a stupefying round trip was officially dead.

The starship was foreign.

"Wonder what they have?" Marconi muttered.

"Trader!" Ross sneered ponderously. He was feeling better; the weight of depression had been lifted for the time being, either by his confession or the electric atmosphere. If every day were like this, he thought vaguely. . . .

"Let's not kid each other," Marconi was saying exuberantly. "This is an event, man! Where are they from, what are they peddling? Do I get a good cut at their wares? It could be fifty thousand shields for me in commission alone. Lurline and I could build a tower house on Great Blue Lake with that kind of money, with a whole floor for her parents! Ross, you just don't know what it is to really be in love. Everything changes."

A jeep roared up and slammed to a stop; Ross blinked and yelled: "Here it comes!"

They watched the ground-controlled approach with the interest of semiprofessionals and concealed their rising excitement with shop talk.

"Whups! There goes the high-power job into action." Marconi pointed as a huge dish antenna swiveled ponderously on its mast. "Seems the medium-output dishes can't handle her."

"Maybe the high-power dish can't either. She might be just plain shot."

"Standard, sealed GCA doesn't get shot, my young friend. Not in a neon-atmosphere tank it doesn't."

"Maybe along about the fifth generation they forgot what it was and cut it open with an acetylene torch to see what was inside."

"Bad luck for us in that case, Ross." The ship steadied on a due-west course and flashed across the heavens and over the horizon.

"Somebody decided a braking ellipse or two was in order. What about line of sight?"

"No sweat. The GCA jockey—and I'd bet it's Delafield himself—pushes a button that hooks him into the high-power dish at every rocket field on Halsey's. It's been all thought out. There's a potential fortune aboard that longliner and Fields Administration wants its percentage for servicing and accommodating."

"Wonder what they have?"

"I already asked that one, Ross."

"So you did."

They lapsed into silence until the rocket boomed in again from the east, high and slow. The big dish swiveled abruptly and began tracking again.

"He'll try to bring her down this time. Yes! There go fore and stabilizing jets."

Flame jutted from the silvery speck high in the blue; its apparent speed slowed to a crawl. It vanished for a second as steering jets turned her slowly endwise. They caught sight of the stern jets when they blasted for the descent.

It was uneventful—just the landing of a very, very big rocket. When a landing is successful it is like every other successful landing ever made.

But the action that the field whirled into immediately following the landing was far from routine. The bullhorns roared that all traders, wipers, rubbernecks, and visitors were to get behind the ready lines and stay there. All Class-Three-and-higher Field personnel were to take stations for longliner clearance. The weapons and decontamination parties were to take their stations immediately. Captain Delafield would issue all future orders and don't let any of the traders talk you out of it, men. Captain Delafield would issue all future orders personally.

Ross watched in considerable surprise as Field men working with drilled precision broke out half a dozen sleek, needle-nosed guns from an innocent-looking bay of the warehouse and manhandled them into position. From another bay a large pressure tank was hauled and backed against the lock of the starship. Ross could see the station medic bustlingly supervise that, and the hosing of white gunk onto the juncture between tank and ship.

Delafield crossed the stretch from the GCA complex to the tank, vanished into it through a pressure-fitted door and that was that. The tank had no windows.

Ross said to Marconi, wonderingly: "What's all this about? There was Doc Gibbons handling the pressure tank, there was Chunk Blaney rolling out

a God-damned cannon I never knew was there—
how many more little secrets are there that I don't
know about?"

Marconi grinned. "They have gun drill once a
month, my young friend, and they never say a
word about it. Let the right rabble-rouser get hold
of the story and he might sail into office on a
platform of 'Keep the bug-eyed monsters off of
Halsey's Planet.' You have to have reasonable pre-
cautions, military and medical, though—and this
is the straight goods—there's never been any trouble of either variety."

The conversation died and there was a long,
boring hour of nothing. At last Delafield appeared
again. One of the decontamination party ran up in
a jeep with a microphone.

"What'll it be?" Ross demanded. "Alphabetic
order? Or just a rush?"

The announcement floored him. "Representative
of the Haarland Trading Corporation please report
to the decontamination tank."

The representative of Haarland Trading Corporation was Marconi.

"Hell," Ross said bitterly. "Good luck with them,
whoever they are."

Marconi brooded for a moment and then said
gruffly, "Come on along."

"You mean it?"

"Sure. Uh—naturally, Ross, you'll give me your
word not to make any commercial offers or inquir-
ies without my permission."

"Oh. Naturally." They started across the field
and were checked through the ready line, Marconi
cheerfully presenting his identification and vouch-
ing for Ross.

Captain Delafield, at the tank, snapped, "What

are you doing here, Ross? You're Oldham's man. I distinctly said—"

"My responsibility, Captain. Will that do it?" Marconi asked.

Delafield snapped, "It'll be your fundament if Haarland hears about it. Actually it's the damnedest situation—they *asked* for Haarland's."

Marconi looked frightened and his hand involuntarily went to his breast pocket. He swallowed and asked, "Where are they from?"

Delafield grimaced and said, "Home."

Marconi exploded, "Oh, no!"

"That's what they say, it's all I can get out of them. I suppose their trajectory can be analyzed, and there must be logs. We haven't been in the ship yet. Nobody goes in until it gets sprayed, rayed, dusted, and busted down into its component parts. Too many places for nasty little mutant bacteria and viruses to lurk."

"Sure, Captain. 'Home,' eh? They're pretty simple?"

"Happy little morons. Fifteen of them, ranging in age from one month to what looks like a hundred and twenty. All they know is 'home' and 'we wish to see the representative of the Haarland Trading Corporation.' First the old woman said it. Then the next in line—he must be about a hundred—said it. Then a pair of identical twins, fifty-year old women, said it in chorus. Then the rest of them on down to the month-old baby, and I swear to God he tried to say it. Well, you're the Haarland Trading Corporation. Go on in."

2

All of the bodies were naked—tiny body of the tot, shrunken bodies of the ancients, firm and healthy bodies of the grownups. Why should they not be naked? There's no weather in a spaceship. And they had no secrets to hide.

When Ross and Marconi came in through the lock, all of them laughed with pleasure at the sight of strangers—all except the baby, at least. The baby was contentedly nursing at the breast of a handsome, laughing woman.

It was the laughter that unnerved Ross. It was cheerful. It had no meanness in it. It reminded him of the happy yelping of puppies at play with a red rubber bone.

It reminded him of his long-ago marriage.

A stab went through him as he made the connection. The simple, mindless pleasure of these empty and happy creatures. The rosy good nature of his wife of a decade past. Ross studied them with mounting unease. Was there a physical resemblance? He tried to find his ex-wife's features in their features, her figure in theirs. And failed. Yet they reminded him inescapably of his miserable year with that half-a-woman. They were physically no kin of hers. They were just cheerful laughers who he knew were less than human.

Like the woman who had been his wife.

The cheerful laughers exposed unblemished teeth in all their mouths, including that of the hundred-and-twenty-year-old matriarch. Why not? If you put calcium and fluorides into a closed system, they stay there.

The old woman stopped laughing at them long enough to say to Marconi, in perfect speech, "We wish to see the representative of the Haarland——"

"Yes, I know. I'm the representative of the Haarland Trading Corporation. Welcome to Halsey's Planet. May I ask what your name is, ma'am?"

"Ma," she said genially.

"Pleased to meet you, Ma. My name's Marconi."

Ma said, bewildered, "You just said you were the representative of the Haarland Trading——"

"Yes, Ma, but that's all right. Let's say that's my other name. Two names—understand?"

She laughed at the idea of two names, wonderingly.

Marconi pressed, "And what's the name of this gentleman?"

"He isn't Gentleman. He's Sonny."

Sonny was a hundred years old.

"Pleased to meet you, Sonny. And your name, sir?"

"Sonny," said a redheaded man of eighty or thereabouts.

The identical-twin women were named The Kids. The baby was named Him. The rest of the troop were named Girl, Ma, or Sonny. After introductions Ross noticed that Him had been passed to another Ma who was placidly suckling him. She had milk; it dribbled from the corner of the baby's mouth. "There isn't another baby left in the ship, is there?" Ross asked in alarm.

They laughed and the Ma suckling the baby said: "There was, but she died. Mostly they do when you put them into the box after they get born. Ma here was lucky. Her Him didn't die."

"Put them in the box? What box? Why?"

Marconi was nudging him fiercely in the ribs. He ignored it.

They laughed amiably at his ignorance and explained that the box was the box, and that you put your newborn babies into it because you put your newborn babies into it.

A beep tone sounded from the ship.

Ma said, "We have to go back now, The Representative of the Haarland Trading Corporation Marconi."

"What for?"

Ma took a deep breath and said rapidly, "At regular intervals signaled by a tone of six hundred cycles and an intermittent downward shifting of the ship lights from standard illumination frequency to a signal frequency of 420 millimicrons, ship's operating personnel take up positions at the control boards for recalibration of ship-working meters and instruments against the battery of standard meters. We'll be right back."

They trooped through the hatch, laughing, to leave Ross and Marconi staring at each other in the decontamination tank.

Ross whispered, "Somebody planned this. All of it."

"Well, of course someone planned it! Planned it beautifully! Even after a dozen centuries, it still *works.*"

Ross stared at the little man. "It works? But it's running down, Marconi, can't you see that? Like Ghost Town. Like us! And you've known about all this all along." Marconi gazed back at him across the unbridgeable gap of four grades of seniority. He didn't answer. He shrugged angrily. "Well," Ross said slowly, "at last I know why the Longliner Departments have their little secrets. 'The Box,' I say it's murder."

"Be reasonable," Marconi told him—but his own face was white under the glaring germicidal lamps. "You can't let them increase without limit or they'd all die. And before they died there'd be cannibalism. Which do you prefer?"

"Letting kids be born and then snuffing them out if a computer decides they're the wrong sex or over the quota is inhuman."

"I didn't say I like it, Ross. But it works."

"So do pills!"

"Pills are a private matter. A person might privately decide not to take hers. The box is a public matter and the group outnumbers and overrules a mother who decides not to use it. There's your question of effectiveness answered, but there's another point. Those people are sane, Ross. Preposterously naive, but sane! Saner than childless women or sour old bachelors we both know who never had to love anything small and helpless, and so come to love nobody but themselves. They're sane. Partly because the women get a periodic biochemical shakeup called pregnancy that their biochemical balance is designed to mesh with. Partly because the men find tenderness and protectiveness in themselves toward the pregnant women. Mostly, I think, because—it's something to do.

"Can you imagine the awful monotony of life in the ship? The work is sheer rote and repetition. They can't read or watch screentapes. They were born in the ship, and the books and screentapes are meaningless because they know nothing to compare them with. The only change they see is each other, aging toward death. Frequent pregnancies are a Godsend to them. They compare and discuss them; they wonder who the fathers are; they make bets on rations; the men brag and keep score. The girls look forward to their first and their last. The jokes they make up about them! The way they speculate about twins! The purgative fear, even, keeps them sane."

"And then," Ross said, " 'the box.' "

Staring straight ahead at the ship's port Marconi echoed: "Yes. 'The box.' If there were another way—but there isn't."

His breezy young boss, Charles Oldham IV, was not pleased with what Ross had to report.

"Asked for Haarland!" he repeated unbelievingly. "Those dummies didn't know where they were going or where they were from, but they knew enough to ask for Haarland." He slammed a ruler on his desk and yelled: "God-damn it! A long-term mnemonic command! That's unfair trading practice!"

"Mr. Oldham!" Ross protested, aghast. For a superior to lose his temper publicly was unthinkable; it covered you with embarrassment.

"Manners be God-damned too!" Oldham screamed, breaking up fast. "What do you know about the

state of our books? What do you know about the
overhead I inherited from my loving father? What
the hell do you know about the downcurve in
sales?"

"These fluctuations—" Ross began soothingly.

"Fluctuations be God-damned! I know a fluctua-
tion when I see one, and I know a long-term down-
trend when I see one. And that's what we're riding,
right into bankruptcy, fellow. And now these God-
damned dummies blow in from nowhere with a
consignment exclusively for Haarland—I don't know
why I don't get the hell out of this stupid business
and go live in a shack on Great Blue Lake and let
the planet go ahead and rot."

Ross's horror at the unseemly outburst was
eclipsed by his interest at noting how similarly he
and Oldham had been thinking. "Sir," he ventured, "I've had something on my mind for a
while—"

"It can wait," Oldham growled, collecting himself with a visible effort. So there went Ross's
chance to resign. "What about customs? I know
Haarland hasn't got enough cash to lay out. Who
has?"

Ross said glibly: "Usual arrangement, sir. They
turn an estimated twenty-five per cent of the cargo
over to the port authority for auction, the receipts
to be in full discharge of their import tax. And
I suppose they enter protective bids. They aren't
wasting any time—auction's 2100 tonight."

"You handle it," Oldham muttered. "Don't go
over one hundred thousand shields. Diversify the
purchases as much as possible. And try to sneak
some advance information out of the dummies if
you get a chance."

"Yes, sir," Ross said. As he left he saw Oldham taking a plastic bottle from a wall cabinet.

And that, thought Ross as he rode to the Free Port, was the first crack he had ever seen in the determined optimism of the trading firm's top level. They were optimists and they were idealists, at least to hear them tell it. Interplanetary trading was a cause and a mission; the traders kept the flame of commerce alight. Perhaps, thought Ross, they had been able to indulge in the hypocrisy of idealism only so long as a population upcurve assured them of an expanding market. Perhaps now that births were flattening out—some said the dirty word "declining"—they all would drop their optimistic creed in favor of fang-and-claw competition for the favors of the dwindling pool of consumers.

And that, Ross thought gloomily, was the way he'd go himself if he stayed on: junior trader, to senior trader, to master trader, growing every year more paranoidally suspicious of his peers, less scrupulous in the chase of the shield. . . .

But he was getting out, of course. The purser's berth awaited. And then, perhaps, the awful depressions he had been enduring would lift off him. He thought of the master traders he knew: his own man Oldham, none too happy in the hereditary business; Leverett, still smug and fat with his terrific windfall of the Sirius IV starship fifteen years ago; Marconi's boss Haarland—Haarland broke the sequence all to hell. It just wasn't possible to think of Haarland being driven by avarice and fear. He was the oldest of them all, but there was more zest and drive in this parchment body than in all the rest of them combined. Ross wondered for a moment what it could be like to work for a man like Haarland, so different from his own boss. Of course

the thing was impossible. You signed on with a
trading firm, you stayed with that trading firm.
You couldn't change masters. There were too many
trade secrets; how could the system survive if a
clerk from Leverett could take his privy knowledge to, say, an Oldham's?

And certainly the system survived. Fraying at
the edges, running down, wearing out—but it
survived.

Still, old man Haarland was a wild card in the
deck. He had other things in his mind than profit,
whatever those other things were.

They were secrets, of course.

When you came down to it, there were only two
kinds of people on Halsey's Planet. The kind who
had secrets locked inside their minds. And the
kind who had nothing at all.

The auction hall had run down, too. It had been
built to serve as a great planetary trading pit, with
room for scores or hundreds of hard-driving specu-
lators. Now there were hardly a dozen that mattered. Ross found a seat near the velvet ropes. One
of the professional bidders lounging against a wall
flicked him an almost imperceptible signal, and he
answered with another. That was that; he had his
man, and a good one. They had often worked together in the commodity pits, but not so often or
so exclusively that the bidder would be instantly
known as his.

Inside the enclosure Marconi, seated at a bare
table, labored over a sheaf of papers with one of
the "Sonnies" from the ship. Sonny was wriggling
in coveralls, the first clothes he had ever worn.
Ross saw they hadn't been able to get shoes onto
him.

Who else did he know? Captain Delafield was sitting somberly within the enclosure; Win Fraley, the hottest auctioneer of the Port, was studying a list, his lips moving. Every trading firm was represented; the heads of the smaller firms were there in person, not daring to delegate the bidding job. Plenty of Port personnel, just there for the excitement of the first longliner in fifteen years, even though it was well after close of the business day.

The goods were in sealed cases against the back wall as usual. Ross could only tell that some of them were perforated and therefore ought to contain living animals. Only the one Sonny from the starship crew was there; presumably the rest were back on the ship. He wouldn't be able to follow Oldham's orders to snoop out the nature of the freight from them. Well, damn Oldham; damn even the auction, Ross thought to himself. His mood of gloom did not lift.

The auction was a kind of letdown. All that turmoil and bustle, concentrated in a tiny arc around the velvet ropes, contrasted unpleasantly with the long, vacant rows of dusty seats that stretched to the back of the hall. Maybe a couple of centuries ago Ross would have enjoyed the auction more. But now all it made him think of was the thing he had been brooding about for a night and a day, the slow emptying of the planet, the. . . .

Decay.

But, as usual, no one else seemed to notice or to care.

Captain Delafield consulted his watch and stood up. He rapped the table. "In accordance with the rules of the Trade Commission and the appropriate governing statutes," he droned, "certain merchandise will now be placed on public auction.

The Haarland Trading Corporation, consignee, agrees and consents to divest itself of merchandise from Consignment 97-W amounting by estimate of the customs authorities to twenty-five per cent of the total value of all merchandise in said consignment. All receipts of this auction are to be entered as excise duties paid by the consignee on said merchandise, said receipts to constitute payment in full on excise of Consignment 97-W. The clerk will record; if any person here present wishes to enter an objection let him do so thank you." He glanced at a slip of paper in his hand. "I am requested to inform you that the Haarland Trading Corporation has entered with the clerk a protective bid of five thousand shields on each item." There was a rustle in the hall. Five thousand shields was a lot of money. "Your auctioneer, Win Fraley," said Captain Delafield, and sat down in the first row of seats.

The auctioneer took a long, slow swallow of water, his eyes gleaming above the glass at the audience. Theatrically he tossed the glass to an assistant, smacked his hands together and grinned. "Well," he boomed genially, "I don't have to tell you gentlemen that somebody's going to get rich tonight. Who knows—maybe it'll be you? But you can't make money without spending money, so without any further ado, let's get started. I have here," he rapped out briskly, "Item Number One. Now you don't know and I don't know exactly what Item Number One contains, but I can tell you this, they wouldn't have sent it two hundred and thirty-one lights if they didn't think it was worth something. Let's get this started with a rush, folks, and I mean with a big bid to get in the right mood. After all, the more you spend here the less you have to pay in taxes," he laughed. "You ready? Here's the dope. Item Number One——" His assistant slapped a carton at the extreme left of the line. "——weight two hundred and fifteen grams, net; fifteen cubic centimeters; one microfilm reel included. Reminds me," he reminisced, "of an item just about that size on the Sirius IV shipment. Turned out to be Maryjane seeds, and I don't suppose I have to tell anybody here how much Mr. Leverett made out of Maryjanes; I bet every one of us has been smoking them ever since. What do you say, Mr. Leverett? You did all right last time—want to say ten thousand as a first big bid on Item Number One? Nine thousand? Do I hear——?"

One of the smaller traders, not working through a professional bidder, not even decently delegating the work to a junior, bid seventy-five hundred shields. Like the spokesmen for the other big traders, Ross sat on his hands during the early stages. Let the small fry give themselves a thrill and drop out. The big firms knew to a fraction of a shield how much the small ones could afford to bid on a blind purchase, and the easiest way to handle them was to let them spend their budgets in a hurry. Of course the small traders knew all this, and their strategy, when they could manage it, was to hold back as long as possible. It was a matter of sensing emotion rather than counting costs; of recognizing the fraction of a second in which a little fellow made up his mind to acquire an item and bidding him up—of knowing when he'd gone his limit and letting him have it at a ruinous price. It was an art, and Ross, despising it, knew that he did it very, very well.

He yawned and pretended to read a magazine while the first six items went on the block; the little traders seemed desperate enough to force the price up without help. He bid on Item Seven partly to squeeze a runt trader and partly to test his liaison with his professional bidder. It was perfect; the pro caught his signal—a bored inspection of his fingernails—while seeming to peek clumsily at the man from Leverett's.

Ross let the next two pass and then acquired three items in rapid succession. The fever had spread to most of the bidders by then; they were starting at ten thousand and up. One or two of the early birds had spent their budgets and were leaving, looking sandbagged—as indeed they had been. Ross signaled "take five" to his professional and strolled out for a cup of coffee.

On the way back he stopped for a moment outside the hall to look at the stars and breath. There were the familiar constellations—The Plowman, the Rocket Fleet, Marilyn Monroe. He stood smoking a cigarette and yearning toward them until somebody moved in the darkness near him. "Nice night, Ross," the man said gloomily.

It was Captain Delafield. "Oh, hello, sir," Ross said, the world descending around him again like a too-substantial curtain. "Taking a breather?"

"Had to," the captain growled. "Ten more minutes in that place and I would have thrown up. Damned money-grabbing traders. No offense, Ross; just that I don't see how you stand the life. Seems to have got worse in my time. Much worse. You high-rollers goading the pee-wees into shooting their wads—it didn't use to be like that. We had gallantry. We didn't stomp a downed man. I don't see how you stand it."

"I can't stand it," Ross said quietly. "Captain Delafield, you don't know—I'm so sick to death of the life I'm leading and the work I'm doing that I'd do anything to get away. Mr. Fallon offered me a purser's spot on his ship; I've been thinking about it very seriously."

"Purser? A dirty job. There's nothing to do except when you're in port, and then there's so much to do that you never get to see the planet. I don't recommend it, Ross."

Ross grunted, thinking. If even the purser's berth was no way out, what was left for him? Sixty more years of waiting for a starship and scheming how to make a profit from its contents? Sixty more years watching Ghost Town grow by nibbles on Halsey City, watching the traders wax in savagery as they battled for the ever-diminishing pool of consumers, watching obscene comedies like Lurline of the Old Landowners graciously consenting to wed Marconi of the New Nobodies? He said wearily: "Then what shall I do, Captain? Rot here with the rest of the planet?"

Delafield shrugged, surprisingly gentle. "You feel it too, Ross? I'm glad to hear it. I'm not sensitive, thank God, but I know they talk about me. They say I quit the space-going fleet as soon as I had a chance to grab off the port captaincy. They're right; I did. Because I was frightened."

"Frightened? You?" Delafield's ribbons for a dozen heroic rescues gleamed in the light that escaped from the hall.

"Sure, Ross." He flicked the ribbons. "Each one of these means I and my men pulled some people out of a jam they got into because of somebody's damned stupidity or slow reflexes or defective memory. No; I withdraw that. The Thetis got stove in because of mechanical failure, but all the rest were human error. There got to be too many for me; I want to enjoy my old age.

"Ready to face that if you become a purser? I can tell you that if you don't like it here you won't be happy on Sunward and you won't like the moons. And you most especially and particularly won't like being a purser. It's the same job you're doing now, but it pays less, offers you a six-by-eight cubicle to work and live in, and gives you nothing resembling a future to aim at. Now if you'll excuse me, I'd better get back inside. I've enjoyed our talk."

Ross followed the captain gloomily. Nothing had changed inside; Ross lounged in the doorway inconspicuously picking up the eye of his bidder. Marconi was gone from the enclosure. Ross looked around hopefully and found his friend in agitated conversation with an unrecognizable but also agitated man at the back of the hall. Ross drifted over. Heads were turning in the front rows. As Ross got within range he heard a couple of phrases. "—in the ship. Mr. Haarland specially asked for you. Please, Mr. Marconi!"

"Oh, hell," Marconi said disgustedly. "Go on. Tell him I'll be there. But how he expects me to take care of things here and—" He trailed off as he caught sight of Ross.

"Trouble?" Ross asked.

"Not exactly. The hell with it." Marconi stared indecisively at the auctioneer for a moment. He said obscurely, "Taking your life isn't enough; he wants more. And I thought I'd be able to see Lurline tonight. Excuse me, Ross. I've got to get over to the ship." He hurried out.

Ross looked wonderingly after him, caught the eye of his bidder, and went back to work. By the

time the auction was over and dawn was breaking in the west, Oldham Trading had bought nine
lots of merchandise: three breathing, five flowering,
and one a roll of microfilm. Ross took his prizes to
the office where Charles Oldham was waiting, much
the better for a few drinks and a long nap.

"How much?" demanded Oldham. Evidently they
were both supposed to ignore his hysterical outburst of the night before.

"Fifty-seven thousand total," said Ross.

"For nine lots? Good man, Ross! That's wonderful. With any kind of luck at all we'll have a hell of
a year. Rule of Eight, you know." The Rule of
Eight said that of every eight imports four were
going to be worthless, one would be good stuff but
unfortunately duplicating something already on
the market, two would barely pay expenses—but
the one that took off would take off big enough to
pay for all. "There ought to be a fat bo— There
ought to be a bonus in it for you, Ross," he babbled, beginning to grow maudlin. Evidently there
had been more than a few drinks. "Stick around!
We'll view the microfilm. We'll get a zoologist and
a botanist in to assess the organics. We'll talk
marketing strategies. We'll—"

"I'm dead," said Ross. "Another time, all right?"

Oldham looked surprised. Then he looked of-
fended. There wasn't likely to be another time like
this for ten years at least, and both of them knew
it. But he ended up suddenly conciliatory to the
wonderful young up-and-comer who had bid in all
this merchandise at such a whopping bargain price.

Ross didn't care anymore.

He dragged himself from the building, into a
cab, through the deserted avenues, home. Morosely
undressing, he lit a cigarette and brooded. Well,

that was it. The Big One. The day you dreamed of
since first you became an apprentice. The day a
longliner came to port, with all the mystery and
majesty of the unknown reaches of interstellar
space. It came. You had the alien prizes in your
hands. You saw how tawdry a triumph it was, as
sleazy as the gimcracks you exported every day to
Sunward, and the taste in your mouth was the dry
taste of dust.

The taste of decay.

He stared out of the window, over the sagging
roofs of Ghost Town to the distant Yards. What a
day this day had been! What mysteries explained,
and new mysteries discovered! And why was it that
every answer, always, generated two new questions?

The sun was high over the surrounding moun-
tains. He caught a glimpse of light that, he was
nearly sure, was the reflected gleam of the longliner
starship, towering over all else in the Yards. Was
Marconi there inside it? And what was he doing
there? What had old man Haarland called him to
the ship for? What was Marconi frightened and
belligerent about?

So many questions. . . .

Ross stubbed out his cigarette. It tasted—decayed.

At least he would have no trouble sleeping. He
wouldn't toss and turn, agonizing over the really
very trivial question of whether or not he should
quit his job. He fell asleep remembering what
Delafield had told him about Sunward and the
moons. His dreams were of cities on another
planet—a planet of another star—a planet with
alien cities and wondrous artifacts, and every one
of them populated with aloof Oldhams, avaricious
Marconis, and giggling, grinning imbeciles who all
wore his own face.

3

"Wake up, Ross," Marconi was saying, joggling him. "Come on, wake up."

Ross thrust himself up on an elbow and opened his eyes. He said with a tongue the size of his forearm in a dust-lined mouth: "Wha' time is it? Wha' the hell are you doing here, for that matter?"

"It's around noon. You've slept for three hours; you can get up."

"Uh." Ross automatically reached for a cigarette. The smoke got in his eyes and he rubbed them; the cigarette dehydrated and seared what little healthy tissue appeared to be left in his mouth. But it woke him up a little. "What are you doing here?" he demanded.

Marconi's hand was involuntarily on his breast pocket again, the one in which he carried Lurline's picture. He said harshly: "You want a job? Topside? Better than purser?" He wasn't meeting Ross's eye. His gaze roved around the apartment and lighted on a coffee maker. He filled it and snapped it on. "Get dressed, will you?" he demanded.

Ross sat up. "What's this all about, Marconi? What do you want, anyway?"

Marconi, for his own reasons, became violently angry. "You're the damnedest question-asker I ever did meet, Ross. I'm trying to do you a favor."

"What favor?" Ross asked suspiciously.

"You'll find out. You've been bellyaching to me long enough about how dull your poor little life is. Well, I'm offering you a chance to do something big and different. And what do you do? You crawfish. Are you interested or aren't you? I told you: It's a space job, and a big one. Bigger than being a purser for Fallon. Bigger than you can imagine."

Ross began to struggle into his clothes, no more than half comprehending, but stimulated by the magic words. He asked, puzzling sleepily over what Marconi had said, "What are you sore about?" His guess was that Lurline had broken a date—but it seemed to be the wrong time of day for that.

"Nothing," Marconi said grumpily. "Only I have my own life to live." He poured two cups of coffee. He wouldn't answer questions while they sipped the scalding stuff. But somehow Ross was not surprised when, downstairs, Marconi headed his car along the winding road through Ghost Town that led to the Yards.

Every muscle of Ross's body was stiff and creaky; another six hours of sleep would have been a wonderful thing. But as they roared through the rutted streets of Ghost Town he began to feel alive again. He stared out the window at the flashing ruins, piecing together the things Marconi had said.

"Watch it!" he yelled, and Marconi swerved the car around a tumbled wall. Ross was shaking, but

Marconi only drove faster. This was crazy! You didn't race through Ghost Town as though you were on the pleasure parkways around the Great Blue Lake; it wasn't safe. The buildings had to fall over from time to time—nobody, certainly, bothered to keep them in repair. And nobody bothered to pick up the pieces when they fell, either, until the infrequent road-mending teams made their rounds.

But at last they were out of Ghost Town, on the broad highway from Halsey City to the port. The administration building and car park was just ahead.

It was there that Marconi spoke again. "I'm assuming, Ross, that you weren't snowing me when you said you wanted thrills, chills, and change galore."

"That's not the way I put it. But I wasn't snowing you."

"You'll get them. Come on."

He led Ross across the field to the longliner, past a gaggle of laughing, chattering Sonnies and Mas. He ignored them.

The longliner was a giant of a ship, a blunt torpedo a hundred meters tall. It had no ports—naturally enough; the designers of the ship certainly didn't find any reason for its idiot crew to look out into space, and landings and takeoffs would be remote-controlled. Hundreds of years old it was; but its metal was as bright, its edges as sharp, as the newest of the moon freighters at the other end of the hardstand. Hundreds of years—a long trip, but an almost unimaginably long distance that trip covered. For the star that spawned it was as far away as light would travel in two centuries and a bit. At 186,000 miles per second, sixty sec-

onds in a minute, sixty minutes in an hour. . . .
Ross's imagination gave up the task. It was far.

He stared about him in fascination as they entered the ship. He gaped at sterile, gray-walled
cubicles, each of which contained the same chair
and cot—no screen or projector for longliners. Ross
remembered his rash words of the day before about
shipping out on a longliner, and shuddered.

"Here we are," said Marconi, stopping before a
closed door. He knocked and entered.

It was a cubicle like the others, but there were
reels stacked on the floor and a projector. Sitting
on the cot in a just-awakened attitude was old
man Haarland himself. To Ross he looked beady-
eyed. Watchful. And really, when you thought about
it, out of place. What was he doing in this ship?
True, it belonged to him, at least by courtesy.
Longliners were the property of the trader who
won their contents, though seldom were they worth
more than scrap value. No one would relaunch a
longliner.

The old man was measuring Ross with a steady
and penetrating gaze. Tone neutral, he said, "This
is Ross?"

"Yes, sir," said Marconi. There was tension in
his voice and posture. "Sir? Do you want me to
stay while you, uh, do the, uh, interview?"

"Good God, no," growled Haarland. "Get out.
Sit down, Ross."

Ross sat down. Marconi, carefully looking neither to right nor to left, also obeyed orders. He
closed the door behind him. Haarland stretched,
scratched and yawned. "I'm getting too old for
this," he said. "You're Ross."

There seemed no good way to deny it. "Yes, sir."

"Um. Marconi thinks a lot of you. He tells me

you're quite a fellow—sincere, competent, a good man to give a tough job to. Namely, his."

"His job? Junior-Fourth Trader? You're going to make me a Junior-Fourth Trader?"

"God, no! Something a lot more challenging than that! But first I have to ask you some questions. I'm told you were ready to quit Oldham for a purser's berth. That's ethical. Would you consider it unethical to quit Oldham for Haarland?"

"Yes—I think I would."

"Glad to hear it! What if the work had absolutely nothing to do with trading and never brings you into a competitive situation with Oldham?"

"Well—" Ross scratched his jaw. "Well, I think that would be all right. But a Junior-Fourth's job, Mr. Haarland—" The floor bucked and surged under him. He gasped, "What was that?"

"Blastoff, I imagine," Haarland said calmly. "We're taking off. Better lie down."

Ross flopped to the floor. It was no time to argue, not with the first-stage pumps thundering and the preheaters roaring their threat of an imminent four-G thrust.

It came like thunder, slapping Ross against the floor plates as though he were glued to them. He felt every tiny wrinkle in every weld he lay on, and one arm had fallen across a film reel. He heaved, and succeeded in levering it off the reel. It thwacked to the floor as though sandbags were stacked meters-high atop it.

Blackout came very soon.

He awoke in free fall. He was orbiting aimlessly about the cubicle.

Haarland was strapped to the cot, absorbed in manipulating the portable projector, trying to thread a free-floating film. Ross bumped against the old man; Haarland abstractedly shoved him off.

He careened from a bulkhead and flailed for a grip.

"Oh," said Haarland, looking up. "Awake?"

"Yes, awake!" Ross said bitterly. "What is all this? Where are we?"

The old man said formally, "Please forgive my cavalier treatment of you. You must not blame your friend Marconi; he had no idea that I was planning an immediate blastoff with you. I had an assignment for him which he—he preferred not to accept. Not to mince words, Ross, he quit."

"Quit his job?"

The old man shook his head. "No, Ross. Quit much more than the job of working for me. He quit on an assignment which is—I am sorry if it sounds melodramatic—absolutely vital to the human race." He suddenly frowned. "I—I think," he added weakly. "Bear with me, Ross. I'll try to explain as I go along. But, you see, Marconi left me in the lurch. I needed him and he failed me. He felt that you would be glad to take it on, and he told me something about you." Haarland glowered at Ross and said, with a touch of bitterness, "A recommendation from Marconi, at this particular point, is hardly any recommendation at all. But I haven't much choice—and, besides, I took the liberty of calling that pompous young fool you work for."

"Mister Haarland!" Ross cried, outraged. "Oldham may not be any prize but really—"

"Oh, you know he's a fool. But he had a lot to say about you. Enough so that, if you want the assignment, it's yours. As to the nature of the assignment itself—" Haarland hesitated, then said briskly, "The assignment itself has to do with a message my organization received via this longliner. Yes, a message. You'll see. It has also to do with certain facts I've found in its log which, if I can ever get this damned thing working— There we are."

He had succeeded in threading the film.

He snapped on the projector. On the screen appeared a densely packed block of numerals, rolling up and being replaced by new lines as fast as the eye could take them in. Haarland said, "Notice anything?"

Ross swallowed. "If that stuff is supposed to mean anything to me," he declared, "it doesn't."

Haarland frowned. "But Marconi said— Well, never mind." He snapped off the projector. "That was the ship's log, Ross. It doesn't matter if you can't read it; you wouldn't, I suppose, have had such call for that sort of thing working for Oldham. It is a mathematical description of the routing of this ship, from the time it was space-launched until it arrived here yesterday. It took a long time, Ross. The reason that it took a long time is partly that it came from far away. But, even more, there is another reason. We were not this ship's destination! Not the original destination. We weren't even the first alternate—or the second alternate. To be exact, Ross, we were the seventh choice for this ship."

Ross let go of his stanchion, floated a yard, and flailed back to it. "That's ridiculous, Mr. Haarland," he protested. "Besides, what has all this to do with—"

"Bear with an old man," said Haarland, with an amused gleam in his eye.

There was very little he could do but bear with him, Ross thought sourly. "Go on," he said.

Haarland said professorially, "It is conceivable, of course, that a planet might be asleep at the switch. We could believe it, I suppose, if it seemed that the first-choice planet somehow didn't pick the ship up when this longliner came into radar range. In that event, of course, it would orbit once or twice on automatics, and then select for its first alternate target—which it did. It might be a human failure in the GCA station—once." He nodded earnestly. "Once, Ross. Not six times. No planet passes up a trading ship."

"Mr. Haarland," Ross exploded, "it seems to me that you're contradicting yourself all over the place. Did six planets pass this ship up or didn't six planets pass this ship up? Which is it? And why would anybody pass a longliner up anyhow?"

Haarland asked, "Suppose the planets were vacant?"

"What?" Ross was shaken. "But that's silly! I mean, even I know that the star charts show which planets are inhabited and which aren't."

"And suppose the star charts are wrong? Suppose the planets have become vacant? The people have died off, perhaps; their culture decayed."

Decay. Death and decay.

Ross was silent for a long time. He took a deep breath. He said at last, "Sorry. I won't interrupt again."

Haarland's expression was a weft of triumph and relief. "Six planets passed this ship up. Remember Leverett's ship fifteen years ago? Three planets passed that one before it came to us. So there are nine different planets, all listed on the traditional star charts as inhabited, civilized, equipped with GCA radars, and everything else needed—nine planets which are now out of communication, Ross."

Decay, thought Ross. Aloud he said, "Tell me why."

Haarland shook his head. "No," he said strongly, "I want you to tell me. I'll tell you what I can. I'll tell you the message that this ship brought to me. I'll tell you all I know, all I've told Marconi that he isn't man enough to use, and the things that Marconi will never learn, as well. But why nine planets that used to be pretty much like our own planet are now out of communication, that you'll have to tell me."

Forward rockets boomed; the braking blasts hurled Ross against the forward bulkhead. Haarland rummaged under the cot for spacesuits. He flung one at Ross.

"Put it on," he ordered. "Come to the airlock. I'll show you what you can use to find out the answers." He slid into the pressure suit, dived, weightless down the corridor, Ross zooming after.

They stood in the airlock, helmets sealed. Wordlessly Haarland opened the petcocks, heaved on the lock door. He gestured with an arm.

Floating alongside them was a ship, a ship like none Ross had ever seen before.

4

Picture Leif's longboat bobbing in the swells outside Ambrose Light, while the twentieth-century liners steam past; a tiny, ancient thing, related to the new giants only as the Eohippus resembles the horse.

The ship that Haarland revealed was fully as great a contrast, though the difference in scale went the other way. It was a pygmy. Ross knew spaceships as well as any grounder could, both the lumbering interplanet freighters and the titanic longliners. But the ship that swung around Halsey's Planet was a midget (fueled rocket ships must inevitably be huge); its jets were absurdly tiny, clearly incapable of blasting away from planetary gravity; its entire hull length was unbroken and sheer (did the pilot dare fly blind?).

The coupling connections were being rigged between the ships. "Come aboard," said Haarland, spryly wriggling through the passage. Ross, swallowing his astonishment, followed.

The ship was tiny indeed. When Ross and Haarland, clutching handholds, were drifting weightlessly in its central control cabin, they very nearly filled it. There was one other cabin, Ross saw; and the two compartments accounted for a good nine-tenths of the cubage of the ship. Where that left space for the combustion chambers and the fuel tanks, the crew quarters, and the cargo holds, Ross could not imagine. He said: "All right, Mr. Haarland. Talk."

Haarland grinned toothily, his expression eerie in the flickering violet light that issued from a gutter around the cabin's wall.

"This is a spaceship, Ross. It's a pretty old one—fourteen hundred years, give or take a little. It's not much to look at, compared with the up-to-date models you're used to, but it's got a few features that you won't find on the new ones. For one thing, Ross, it doesn't use rockets." He hesitated. "Ask me what it does use," he admitted, "and I can't tell you. I know the name, because I read it: nucleophoretic drive. What nucleophoresis is and how it works, I can't say. They call it the Wesley Effect, and the tech manual says something about squared miles of acceleration. Does that mean anything to you? No. How could it? But it works, Ross. It works well enough so that this little ship will get you where you're going very quickly. The stars, Ross—it will take you to the stars. Faster than light. What the top speed is I have no idea; but there is a ship's log here, too. And it has a three-month entry—three months, Ross!—in which this little ship explored the solar systems of fourteen stars."

Wide-eyed, Ross held motionless. Haarland paused. "Fourteen hundred years," he repeated.

"Fourteen hundred years this ship has been floating out here. And for all that time, the longliners have been crawling from star to star, while little hidden ships like this one could have carried a thousand times as much goods a million times faster. Maybe the time has come to get the ships out of hiding. I don't know. I want to find out; I want you to find out for me. I'll be specific, Ross. I need a pilot. I'm too old, and Marconi turned it down. Someone has to go out there——" he gestured to the blind hull and the unseen stars beyond—— "and find out why the nine planets are out of communication. Will you do it?"

Ross opened his mouth to speak, and a thousand questions competed for utterance. But what he said, barely aloud, was only: "Yes."

The far-off stars—more than a thousand million of them in our galaxy alone. By far the greatest number of them drifted alone through space, or with only a stellar companion as utterly unlivable by reason of heat and crushing gravity as themselves. Fewer than one in a million had a family of planets, and most even of those could never become a home for human life.

But out of a thousand million, any fraction may be a very large number, and the number of habitable planets was in the hundreds.

Ross had seen the master charts of the inhabited universe often enough to recognize the names as Haarland mentioned them: Tau Ceti II, Earth, the eight inhabitable worlds of Capella. But to realize that this ship—this ship!—had touched down on each of them, and on a hundred more, was beyond astonishment; it was a dream thing, impossible but unquestioned.

Through Haarland's burning, old eyes, Ross

looked back through fourteen centuries to the time
when this ship was a scout vessel for a colonizing
colossus. The lumbering giant drove slowly through
space on its one-way trip from the planet that
built it—was it semi-mythical Earth? The records
were not clear—while the tiny scout probed each
star and solar system as it drew within range.
While the mother ship was covering a few hundred million miles, the scout might flash across
parsecs to scan half a dozen worlds. And when the
scout came back with word of a planet where
humans could survive, they christened it with the
name of the scout's pilot, and the chartroom labored, and the ship's officers gave orders, and the
giant's nose swerved through a half a degree and
began its long, slow deceleration.

"Why slow?" Ross demanded. "Why not use the
faster-than-light drive for the big ships?"

Haarland grimaced. "Wait, Ross," he said. "Let
me tell it my way. Anyway, that's what this ship
was: a faster-than-light scout ship for a real
longliner. What happened to the longliner the records don't show; my guess is the colonists canni-
balized it to get a start in constructing homes for
themselves. But the scout ship was exempted. The
captain of the expedition had it put in an orbit out
here, and left alone.

"That captain was my ancestor.

"So this ship has been my family's secret ever
since. It's been used a little bit, now and then—my
great-grandfather's father went clear to 40 Eridani
when my great-grandfather was a little boy, but
by and large it has been left alone. It had to be,
Ross. For one thing, it's dangerous to the man who
pilots it. For another, it's dangerous to—the Galaxy."

Haarland's view was anthropomorphic; the danger was not to the immense and uncaring galaxy, but to the sparse fester of life that called itself humanity.

When the race abandoned Earth, it was a gesture of revulsion. Behind them they left a planet that had decimated itself in wars; ahead lay a cosmos that, in all their searches, had revealed no truly sentient life.

Earth was a crippled world, the victim of its playing with nuclear fission and fusion. But the techniques that gave them a faster-than-light drive gave them as well a weapon that threatened solar systems, not cities; that could detonate a sun as readily as atomic bombs could destroy a building. The child with his forbidden matches was now sitting atop a munitions dump; the danger was no longer a seared hand or blinded eye, but annihilation.

And the decision had been made: secrecy. By what condign struggles the secrecy had been enforced, the secrecy itself concealed. But it had worked. Once the radiating colonizers had reached their goals, the nucleophoretic effect had been obliterated from their records and, except for a single man on each planet, from their minds.

Why the single man? Why not bury it entirely?

Haarland said slowly, "There was always the chance that something would go wrong, you see. And—it has."

Ross said hesitantly, "You mean the nine planets that have gone out of communication?"

Haarland nodded. "Do you understand it now?" he asked.

Ross shook his head dizzily. "I'm trying," he said. "This little ship—it travels faster than light. It has been circling out here—how long? Fourteen hundred years? And you kept it secret—you and your ancestors before you—because you were afraid it might be used in war?" He was frowning.

"Not 'afraid' it would be used," Haarland corrected gently. "We knew it would be used."

Ross grimaced. "Well, why tell me about it now? Do you expect me to keep it secret all the rest of my life?"

"I think you would," Haarland said soberly.

"But suppose I didn't? Suppose I blabbed all over the Galaxy, and it was used in war?"

Haarland's face was suddenly, queerly gray. He said, almost to himself, "It seems that there are things worse than war." Abruptly he smiled. "Let's find Ma."

They returned through the coupling and searched the longliner for the old woman. A Sonny told them, "Ma usually hangs around the meter room. Likes to see them blinking." And there they found her.

"Hello, Haarland," she smiled, flashing her superb teeth. "Did you find what you were looking for?"

"Perfect, Ma. I want to talk to you under the seal."

She looked at Ross. "Him?" she asked.

"I vouch for him," Haarland said gravely. "Wesley."

She answered, "The limiting velocity is C."

"But C^2 is not a velocity," Haarland said. He turned to Ross. "Sorry to make a mystery," he apologized. "It's a recognition formula. It identifies one member of what we call the Wesley families, or its messenger, to another. And these people are messengers. They were dispatched a couple of centuries ago by a Wesley family whose ship, for some reason, no longer could be used. Why?—I don't know why. Try your luck, maybe you can figure it out. Ma, tell us the history again."

She knitted her brows and began to chant slowly:

> In great-grandfather's time the target was
>   Clyde,
> Rocketry firm and ores on the side.
> If we hadn't seen them direct we'd of missed
>   'em;
> There wasn't a blip from the whole damn
>   system.
>   That was the first.
> Before great-grandfather's day was done
> We cut the orbit of Cyrnus One.
> The contact there was Trader McCue,
> But the sons o' bitches missed us too.
>   That was the second.
> My grandpa lived to see the green
> Of Target Three through the high-powered
>   screen.
> But where in hell was Builder Carruthers?
> They let us go by like all the others.
>   That was the——"

"Ma," said Haarland. "Thanks very much, but would you skip to the last one?"

Ma grinned.

> The Haarland Trading Corp, was last
> With the fuel down low and going fast.
> I'm glad it was me who saw the day
> When they brought us down on GCA.
> I told him the message; he called it a mystery,
> But anyway this is the end of the history.
>   And it's about time!

"The message, please," Haarland said broodingly.

Ma took a deep breath and rattled off: "L-sub-T equals L-sub-zero e to the minus-T-over-two-N."

Ross gaped. "That's the message?"

"Used to be more to it," Ma said cheerfully. "That's all there is now, though. The darn thing doesn't rhyme or anything. I guess that's the most important part. Anyway, it's the hardest."

"It's not as bad as it seems," Haarland told Ross. "I've asked around. It makes a very little sense."

"It does?"

"Well, up to a point," Haarland qualified. "It seems to be a formula in genetics. The notation is peculiar, but it's all explained, of course. It has something to do with gene loss. Now, maybe that means something and maybe it doesn't. But I know something that does mean something: some member of a Wesley family a couple of hundred years ago thought it was important enough to want to get it across to other Wesley families. Something's happening. Let's find out what it is, Ross." The old man suddenly buried his face in his hands. In a cracked voice he mumbled, "Gene loss and war. Gene loss or war. God, I wish somebody would take this right out of my hands—or that I could drop with a heart attack this minute. You ever think of war, Ross?"

Shocked and embarrassed, Ross mumbled some kind of answer. One might think of war, good breeding taught, but one never talked about it.

"You should," the old man said hoarsely. "War is what this faster-than-light secrecy and identification rigmarole is all about. Right now war is impossible—between solar systems, anyhow, and that's what counts. A planet might just barely manage to fit an invading multigeneration expedition at gigantic cost, but it never would. The fruits of victory—loot, political domination, maybe slaves— would never come back to the fitters of the expedition but to their remote descendants. A firm will take a flyer on a commercial deal like that, but no nation would accept a war on any such basis— because a conqueror is a man, and men die. With F-T-L—faster-than-light travel—they might invade Cyrnus or Azor or any of those other tempting dots on the master maps. Why not? Take the marginal population, hop them up with patriotic fervor and lust for booty, and ship them off to pillage and destroy. There's at least a fifty per cent chance of coming out ahead on the investment, isn't there? Much more attractive deal commercially speaking than our present longliners."

Ross had never seen a war. The last on Halsey's planet had been the Peninsular Rebellion about a century and a half ago. Some half a million constitutional psychopathic inferiors had started themselves an ideal society with theocratic trimmings in a remote and unfruitful corner of the planet. Starved and frustrated by an unrealistic moral creed they finally exploded to devastate their neighboring areas and were quickly quarantined by a radioactive zone. They disintegrated internally, massacred their priesthood, and were permitted to disperse. It was regarded as a shameful episode by every dweller on the planet. It wasn't a subject for popular filmreels; if you wanted to find out about the Peninsular Rebellion you went through many successive library doors and signed your name on lists, and were sternly questioned as to your age and scholarly qualifications and reasons for sniffing around such an unsavory mess.

Ross therefore had not the slightest comprehension of Haarland's anxiety. He told him so.

"I hope you're right," was all the old man would say. "I hope you don't learn worse."

The rest was work.

He had the Yard worker's familiarity with conventional rocketry, which saved him from some study of the fine-maneuvering apparatus of the F-T-L craft—but not much. For a week under Haarland's merciless drilling he jetted the ship about its remote area of space, far from the commerce lanes, until the old man grudgingly pronounced himself satisfied.

There were skull-busting sessions with the Wesley Drive, or rather with a first derivative of it, an insane-looking object which you could vaguely describe as a fan-shaped slide rule taller than a man. There were twenty-seven main tracks, analogues of the twenty-seven main geodesics of Wesley Space—whatever they were and whatever that was. Your cursor settings on the main tracks depended on a thirty-two step computation based on the apparent magnitudes of the twenty-seven nearest celestial bodies above a certain mass which varied according to yet another lengthy relationship. Then, having cleared the preliminaries out of the way, you began to solve for your actual setting on the F-T-L drive controls.

Somehow he mastered it, while Haarland, driving himself harder than he drove the youth who was to be his exploring eyes and ears, coached him and cursed him and—somehow!—kept his own complicated affairs going back on Halsey's Planet. When Ross had finally got the theory of the Wesley Drive in some kind of order in his mind, and had learned all there was to learn about the other worlds, and had cut his few important ties with Halsey's Planet, he showed up in Haarland's planet-based office for a final, repetitive briefing.

Marconi was there.

He had trouble meeting Ross's eyes, but his hand-clasp was firm and his voice warmly friendly—and a little envious. "The very best, Ross," he said. "I—I wish——" He hesitated and stammered. He said, in a flood, "Damn it, I should be going! Do a good job, Ross—and I hope you don't hate me." And he left while Ross, disturbed, went in to see old man Haarland.

Haarland spared no time for sentiment. "You're cleared for space flight," he growled. "According to the visa, you're going to Sunward—in case anyone asks you between here and the port. Actually, let's hear where you *are* going."

Ross said promptly, "I am going on a mission of exploration and reconnaissance. My first proposed destination is Ragansworld; second Gemser, third Azor. If I cannot make contact with any of these three planets, I will select planets at random from the master charts until I find some Wesley Drive families somewhere. The contacts for the first three planets are: On Ragansworld, Foley Associates; on Gemser, the Franklin Foundation; on Azor, Cavallo Machine Tool Company. F-T-L contacts on other planets are listed in the appendix to the master charts. The co-ordinates for Ragansworld are——"

"Skip the co-ordinates," mumbled Haarland, rubbing his eyes. "What do you do when you get in contact with a Wesley Drive family?"

Ross hesitated and licked his lips. "I—well, it's a little hard——"

"Dammit," roared Haarland, "I've told you a *thousand* times——"

"Yessir, I know. All I meant was I don't exactly understand what I'm looking for."

"If I knew what you were to look for," Haarland rasped, "I wouldn't have to send you out looking! Can't you get it through your thick head? *Something* is wrong. I don't know what. Maybe I'm crazy for bothering about it—heaven knows, I've got troubles enough right here—but we Haarlands have a tradition of service, and maybe it's so old that we've kind of forgotten just what it's all about. But it's not so old that I've forgotten the family tradition. If I had a son, he'd be doing this. I counted on Marconi to be my son; now all I have left is you. And that's little enough, heaven knows," he finished bitterly.

Ross, wounded, said by rote: "On landing, I will attempt at once to make contact with the local Wesley Drive family, using the recognition codes given me. I will report to them on all the data at hand and suggest the need for action."

Haarland stood up. "All right," he said. "Sorry I snapped at you. Come on; I'll go up to the ship with you."

And that was the way it happened. Ross found himself in the longliner, then with Haarland in the tiny, ancient, faster-than-light ship which had once been tender to the ship that colonized Halsey's Planet. He found himself shaking hands with a red-eyed, suddenly-old Haarland, watching him crawl through the coupling to the longliner, watching the longliner blast away.

He found himself setting up the F-T-L course and throwing in the drive.

5

Ross was lucky—up to a point. The lucky part
was that the second listed inhabited planet was
still inhabited.

He had not quite stopped shuddering from the
first when the approach radar caught him at the
second. The first planet was given in the master
charts as "Ragansworld. Pop. 900,000,000; diam.
9400 m.; mean orbit 0.8 AU," and its coordinates
went on to describe it as the fourth planet of a
small G-type sun. There had been some changes
made at Ragansworld. Like there was no Ragansworld. The co-ordinates now intersected well inside a bright and turbulent gas cloud.

It appeared that suppressing the F-T-L drive had
not quite annihilated war.

But the second planet, Gemser—there, he was
sure, was a world where nothing was seriously
awry. The scanners told the story: green fields,
busy factories. It might be just a tad old-fashioned,

he thought, almost tenderly—look at the smoke that billowed from those chimneys!

But it was not, he was confident, the kind of planet that would have many Ghost Towns.

He left the ship muttering a name to himself: "Franklin Foundation."

When he was greeted by a corporal's guard of dignified and ceremonially dressed men he said the words clearly and with relief. They smiled at him. They welcomed him. They shook his hand and invited him into a red brick bungalow sort of place that seemed to be the local equivalent of an administration building.

"Franklin Foundation, please?" he said, but they were talking into a telephone. He noticed disapprovingly that they didn't seem to go in for the elaborate decontamination procedures of Halsey's Planet, but refrained from judging. Probably there was some perfectly good reason. Perhaps they had long since bred disease resistance into their bloodstreams. Certainly the four men in his party seemed hale and well preserved, though he didn't think even the youngest of them was less than sixty.

"I would like," he said again. "to be put in touch with the Franklin Foundation, please."

"Come right in here," beamed one of the four, and another said:

"Don't worry about a thing." They held the door for him, and he walked into a small and sybaritically furnished room. The second man said, "Just a few questions. Where are you from?"

Ross said simply, "Halsey's Planet," and waited.

Nothing happened, except that all four men nodded comprehendingly, and the questioner made a mark on the sheet of paper. Ross amplified, "Fifty-three light years away. You know—another star?"

"Certainly," the man said briskly. "Your name?"

Ross told him, but with a considerable feeling of deflation. He thought wryly of his own feelings about the longlines and the far stars; he remembered the stir and community excitement that a starship meant back home. Still, Ross told himself, Halsey's Planet might be just a back eddy in the main currents of civilization. Quite possibly on another world—this one, for instance—travelers from the stars were a commonplace. The field hadn't seemed overly busy, though; and there was nothing resembling a spaceship. Unless—he thought with a sudden sense of shock—those rusting hulks clumped together at the edge of the field had once been spaceships.

But that was hardly likely, he reassured himself. You just don't let spaceships rust.

"Sex?" the man asked, and "Age?" "Education?" "Marital status?" The questions went on for more time than Ross quite understood; and they seemed far from relevant questions for the most part; and some of them were hard questions to answer. "Tau quotient?" for instance; Ross blinked and said, with an edge to his voice:

"I don't know what a tau quotient is."

"Put him down as zero," one of the men advised, and the interlocutor nodded happily.

"Working-with-others rating?" he asked, beaming.

Ross said with controlled irritation, "Look, I don't know anything about these ratings. Will you take me to somebody who can put me in touch with the Franklin Foundation?"

The man who was sitting next to him patted him gently on the shoulder. "Just answer the questions," he said comfortably. "Everything will be all right."

Ross flared, "The hell everything will——"

Something with electrified spikes in it hit him on the back of the neck.

Ross yelled and ducked away; the man next to him returned a little rod to his pocket. He smiled at Ross. "Don't feel bad," he said sympathetically. "Go ahead now, answer the questions."

Ross shook his head dazedly. The pain was already leaving his neck, but he felt nauseated by the suddenness and sharpness of it; he could not remember any pain quite like that in his life. He stood up waveringly and said, "Wait a minute, now——"

This time it was the man on the other side, and the pain was about twice as sharp. Ross found himself on the floor, looking up through a haze. The man on his right kept the rod in his hand, and the expression on his face, while in no way angry, was stern. "Bad boy," he said tenderly. "Why don't you want to answer the questions?"

Ross gasped, "God damn it, all I want is to see somebody! Keep your dirty hands off me, you old fools!" And that was a mistake, as he learned in the blessedly few minutes before he passed out completely under the little rods held by the gentle but determined men.

Then he answered all the questions—bound to a chair, with two of the men behind him, when he had regained consciousness. He answered every one, whether he knew the answer or not. They only had to hit him twice.

When they untied him the next morning, Ross had caught on to the local folkways quite well. The fatherly fellow who released him said, "Follow me," and stood back, smiling but with one hand on one of the little rods. And Ross was careful to say:

"Yes, sir!"

They rode in a three-wheeled car, just Ross and the fatherly fellow. Ross had learned his lesson. He didn't speak without being spoken to. He didn't speak at all. He didn't dare even to look out the window of the car until a couple of quickly sneaked peeks brought no more than a benign nod.

There was not much to see. The fields were green enough, to be sure. They were also full of weeds. The smoky factory stacks on the horizon were busy smoking. And there was no visible Ghost Town . . . or, thought Ross glumly, much of anything else of interest. He gazed at a steam-driven harvesting machine (steam-driven!) bumping over a stand of grain, and wondered starkly what old man Haarland had got him into.

He allowed himself a delicious thought of what he would do to Haarland if ever they should meet again. At the moment, that seemed unlikely.

The car turned off the highway, onto a rutted street that paralleled a high board fence. They rolled through a gate and stopped in front of a barracks building. "Inside," smiled the man kindly, and poked Ross toward a bed. "Just wait here," the man said indulgently. "The rest of your group is out at their morning sessions now. When they come in for lunch you can join them. They'll show you what to do."

Ross managed to make himself say, "Thank you, sir."

He sat down on the edge of a springless, nearly linen-less bed and rubbed the back of his neck where those innocent little rods had taught him manners. Rubbing didn't help. He stood up and peered around.

That didn't help much, either. There was nothing to peer at but neat beds and bare walls. It was not the sort of welcome he had expected.

Ross craned his neck at the window, trying to get a glimpse of the road to the spaceport. The port, and his ship, could not be more than five miles away. The miles might as well have been light-years.

So much for Haarland's great humanitarian mission and heroic, world-saving adventure.

Ross flung himself grumpily on the bed, thinking of Wesley families and genetic equations and decay—and how heedlessly a rising young trader named Ross had tossed away a career to pursue a will-o-the-wisp dream. What he needed to do, he told himself urgently, was think, plan, be resourceful. He closed his eyes to think better. . . .

A noise woke him. Coming in the curiously shaped door—all the doors on this planet seemed to be rectangular—was a girl of about nineteen.

She stared at Ross and said, "Oh!" Then she disappeared. There were footsteps and whispers, and more heads appeared and blinked at him and were jerked back.

Ross stood up in wretched apprehension. All of a sudden he was fourteen years old again, and entering a new school where the old hands were giggling and whispering about the new boy. He swore sullenly to himself.

A new face appeared, halted for an inspection of Ross, and walked confidently in. The man was a good forty years old, Ross thought; perhaps a kind of overseer in this institution—whatever kind of institution it was. He approached Ross at a sedate pace, and he was followed through the door in single file by a couple score men and women. They ranged in age, Ross thought wonderingly, from the leader's forty down to the late teens of the girl who had first peered in the door, and now was at the end of the procession.

The leader said, "How old are you?"

"Why, uh——" Ross figured confusedly: this planet's annual orbital period was roughly forty per cent longer than his own; fourteen into his age, multiplied by ten, making his age in their local calculations. . . .

"Why, I'm nineteen of your years old, about. And a half."

"Yes. And what can you do?"

"Look here, sir. I've been through all this once. Why don't you go and ask those gentlemen who brought me here? And can nobody tell me where the Franklin Foundation is?"

The fortyish fellow, with a look of outrage, slapped Ross across the mouth. Ross knocked him down with a roundhouse right.

A girl yelled, "Good for you, Junior!" and jumped like a wildcat into a slim, gray-haired lady, clawing, and slapping. The throng dissolved immediately into a wild melee. Ross, busily fighting off the fortyish fellow and a couple of his stocky buddies, noted only that the scrap was youth against age, whatever it meant.

"How *dare* you?" a voice thundered, and the rioters froze.

A decrepit wreck was standing in the doorway, surrounded by three or four gerontological textbook cases only a little less spavined than he. "Glory," a girl muttered despairingly. "It would be the minister."

"What is the meaning of this brawl?" rolled from the wreck's shriveled lips in a rich basso—no; rolled, Ross noted, from a flat perforated plate on his chest. There was a small, flesh-colored mike slung before his lips. "Who is responsible here?" asked the golden basso.

Ross's fortyish assailant said humbly: "I am, sir. This new fellow here——"

"Manners! Speak when you're spoken to."

Abjectly: "Yes, sir. I'm sorry, sir."

"Silly fools!" the senile wreck hectored them. "I'm going to take no official notice of this since I'm merely passing through. Luckily for you this is no formal inspection. But you've lost your lunch hour with your asinine pranks. Now get back to your work and never let me hear of a disgraceful incident like this again from Junior Unit Twenty-Three."

He swept out with his retinue. Ross noted that some of the younger girls were crying and that the older men and women were glaring at him murderously.

"We'll teach you manners, you pup," the foreman-type said. "You go on the dye vats this afternoon. Any more trouble and you'll miss a few meals."

Ross told him: "Just keep your hands off me, mister."

The foreman-type expanded into a beam of pleasure. "I thought you'd be sensible," he said. "Everybody to the plant, now!" He collared a pretty girl of about Ross's age. "Helena here is working out a bit of insolence on the dye vats herself. She'll show you." The girl stood with downcast eyes. Ross liked her face and wondered about her figure. Whatever it was like, it was covered from neck to knee by a loose shirt. But the older women wore fitted clothes.

The foreman-type led a grand procession through the door. Helena told Ross: "I guess you'd better get in front of me in line. I go here—" She slipped in deftly, and Ross understood a little more of what went on here. The procession was in order of age.

He had determined to drift for a day or two— not that he seemed to have much choice. The Franklin Foundation, supposedly having endured a good many years, would last another week while he explored the baffling mores of this place and found out how to circumvent them and find his way to the keepers of F-T-L on this world. Nobody would go anywhere with his own ship—not without first running up a takeoff setting for the Wesley Drive!

The line filed into a factory whose like Ross had never before seen. He had a fair knowledge of and eye for industrial processes; it was clear that the place was an electri-cable works. But why was the concrete floor dangerously cracked and sloppily patched? Why was the big enameling oven rumbling and stinking? Why were the rolling mills in a far corner unsupplied with guards and big, easy-to-hit emergency cutoffs? Why was the light bad and the air full of lint? Why did the pickling tank fume and make the workers around it cough hackingly? Most pointed of all, why did the dye vats to which Helena led him stink and slop over?

There were grimy signs everywhere, including the isolated bay where braiding cord was dyed the standard code colors. The signs said things like: AGE IS A PRIVILEGE AND NOT A RIGHT. AGE MUST BE EARNED BY WORK. GRATITUDE

IS THE INDEX OF YOUR PROGRESS TO MA-
TURITY.

Helena said girlishly as she took his arm and
hooked him out of the moving line: "Here's Stink-
ville. Believe me, I'm not going to talk back again.
After all, a person's maturity is measured by a
person's acceptance of a person's environment, isn't
it?"

"Yeah," said Ross. "Listen, Helena, have you
ever heard of a place called the Franklin Foundation?"

"No," she said. "First you climb up here—golly!
I don't even know your name."

"Ross."

"All right, Ross. First you climb up here and
make sure the yarn's running over the rollers right;
sometimes it gets twisted around and then it breaks.
Then you take one of the thermometers from the
wall and you check the vat temperature. It says
right on the thermometers what it should be for
the different colors. If it's off you turn that gas tap
up or down, just a little. Then you check the
wringer rolls where the yarn comes out. Watch
your fingers when you do! The yarn comes in different thicknesses on the same thread so you have
to adjust the wringer rolls so too much dye doesn't
get squeezed out. You can tell by the color; it
shouldn't be lighter after it goes through the rolls.
But the yarn shouldn't come through sloppy and
drip dye on the floor while it travels to the
bobbin——"

There was some more, equally uncomplicated.
He took the yellow and green vats; she took the red
and blue. They had worked in the choking stench
and heat for perhaps three hours before Ross finished
one temperature check and descended to adjust a

gas tap. He found Helena, spent and gasping, on the floor, hidden from the rest of the shop by the bulky tanks.

"Heat knock you out?" he asked briskly. "Don't try to talk. I'll tote you over by the wall away from the burners. Maybe we'll catch a little breeze from the windows there." She nodded weakly.

He picked her up without too much trouble, carried her three yards or so to the wall, still isolated from the rest of the shop. She was ripely curved under that loose shirt, he learned. He set her down easily, crouching himself, and did not take his hands away.

It's been a long time, he thought—and she was responding! Whether she knew it or not, there was a drowsy smile on her face and her body moved a little against his hands, pleasurably. She was breathing harder.

Ross did the sensible thing and kissed her.

Wildcat!

Ross reeled back from her fright and anger, his face copiously scratched. "I'm dreadfully sorry," he sputtered. "Please accept my sincerest——"

The flare-up of rage ended; she was sobbing bitterly, leaning against the wall, wailing that nobody had ever treated her like that before, that she'd be set back three years if he told anybody, that she was a good, self-controlled girl and he had no *right* to treat her that way, and what kind of degenerate was he, not yet twenty and going around kissing girls when *everybody* knew you went crazy from it.

He soothed her—from a distance. Her sobbing dropped to a bilious croon as she climbed the ladder to the green vat, tears still on her face, and checked its temperature.

Ross, wondering if he were already crazy from too much kissing of girls, mechanically resumed his duties. But she had responded. And how long had they been working? And wasn't this shift ever going to end?

All the shifts ended in time. But there was a catch to it: There was always another shift. After the afternoon shift on the dye vats came dinner—porridge!—and then came the evening shift on the dye vats, and then sleep. The foreman was lenient, though; he let Ross off the vats after the end of the second day. Then it was kitchen orderly, and only two shifts a day. And besides, you get plenty to eat.

But it was a long, long way, Ross thought sardonically to himself, from the shining pictures he had painted to himself back on Halsey's Planet. Ross the explorer, Ross the hero, Ross the savior of humanity. . . .

Ross, the semipermanent KP.

As day followed day, Ross explored the dimensions of his prison. It didn't take long. There was not much to explore. The men and women of Junior Unit Twenty-Three lived within constricted horizons. Nearly everything that was not compulsory was prohibited. Even talk. Oh, it was perfectly all right to whisper to someone—someone very near one's own age—that it did, after all, look as though it might rain soon. But Ross's worried questions got no answers at all, either out of fear of the consequences or, more often, out of ignorance. Was there a Franklin Foundation on this planet? "Gee, Ross, I wouldn't know *that*." Had any of them ever heard of planets of other stars? "Well, honestly Ross, that's the kind of grown-up thing, you know, that you find all about when you're older."

There was no doubt that the expedition, so far, was a total bust. And it looked like the expedition ended right here, in Junior Unit Twenty-Three. Ross was in a prison from which there was no easy escape as long as he was cursed with youthfulness. . . .

Of course, the implications of that were that there was a perfectly easy escape in time. All he had to do was get old enough to matter, on this insane planet. Ninety, maybe. And then he would be perfectly free to totter out to the spaceport, dragoon a squad of juniors into lifting him into the ship, and take off. . . .

Helena was some help. But only psychologically; she was pleasant company, but neither she nor anyone else in the roster of forty-eight to whom he was permitted to speak had ever heard of the Franklin Foundation, or F-T-L travel, or anything. Helena said, "Wait for Holiday. Maybe one of the grownups will tell you then?"

"Holiday?" Ross slid back and scratched his shoulder blades against the corner of his bed. Helena was sprawled on the floor, half watching a projected picture on the screen at the end of the dormitory.

"Yes. You're lucky, it's only eight days off. That's when Dobermann——" she pointed to the foreman——"graduates; he's the only one this year. And we all move up a step, and the new classes come in, and then we all get everything we want. Well, pretty near," she amended. "We can't do anything *bad*. But you'll see, it's nice."

Then the picture ended, and it was calisthenics time, and then lights out. Forty-eight men and women on their forty-eight bunks—the honor system appeared to work beautifully; there had been no signs of sex play that Ross had been able to see—slept the sleep of the innocent. While Ross, the forty-ninth, lay staring into the dark with rising hope.

In the kitchen the next morning he got more information from Helena. Holiday seemed to be a cross between saturnalia and Boy's Week; for one day of the year the elders slightly relaxed their grip on the reins. On that day alone one could Speak Before Being Spoken To, Interrupt One's Elders, even Leave the Room without Being Excused.

Whee, Ross thought sourly. But still . . .

The foreman, Dobermann, once you learned how to handle him, wasn't such a bad guy. Ross, studying his habits, learned the proper approach and used it. Dobermann's commonest complaint was of irresponsibility—irresponsibility when some thirty-year-old junior was caught sneaking into line ahead of his proper place, irresponsibility when Ross forgot to make his bed before stumbling out in the dark to his kitchen shift, one awful case of irresponsibility when Helena thoughtlessly poured cold water into the cooking vat while it was turned on. There was a sizzle, a crackle, and a puff of steam, and Helena was weeping over a broken heating element.

Dobermann came storming over, and Ross saw his chance. "That is very irresponsible of you, Helena," he said coldly, back to Dobermann but entirely conscious of his presence. "If Junior Unit Twenty-Three was all as irresponsible as you, it would reflect badly on Mr. Dobermann. You don't know how lucky you are that Mr. Dobermann is so kind to you."

Helena's weeping dried up instantly; she gave Ross one furious glance, and lowered her eyes before Dobermann. Dobermann nodded approvingly to Ross as he waded into Helena; it was a memorable tirade, but Ross heard only part of it. He was looking at the cooking vat; it was a simple-minded bit of construction, a spiral of resistance wire around a ceramic core. The core had cracked and one end of the wire was loose; if it could be reconnected, the cracked core shouldn't matter much—the wire was covered with insulation anyhow. He looked up and opened his mouth to say something, then remembered and merely stood looking brightly attentive.

"——looks like you want to go back to the vats," the foreman was finishing. "Well, Helena, if that's what you want we can make you happy. This time you'll be by yourself, too; you won't have Ross to help you out when the going's rough. Will she, Ross?"

"No, sir," Ross said immediately. "Sir?"

Dobermann looked back at him, frowning. "What?"

"I think I can fix this," Ross said modestly.

Dobermann's eyes bulged. "Fix it?"

"Yes, sir. It's only a loose wire. Back where I come from, we all learned how to take care of things like that when we were still in school. It's just a matter of——"

"Now, hold on, Ross!" the foreman howled. "Tampering with a machine is bad enough, but if you're going to turn out to be a liar, too, you're going just too far! School, indeed! You know perfectly well, Ross, that even I won't be ready for school until after Holiday. Ross, I knew you were a troublemaker, knew it the first day I set eyes on you.

School! Well, we'll see how you like the school I'm going to send you to!''

The vats weren't so bad the second time. Even though the porridge was cold for two days, until somebody got around to delivering a different though equally worn-out cooking vat.

Helena passed out from the heat three times. And when, on the third time, Ross, goaded beyond endurance, kissed her again, there were no hysterics.

6

From birth to puberty you were an infant. From puberty to Dobermann's age, a junior. From ten years after that you went to school, learning the things you had neither the need nor the right to know before.

And then you were Of Age.

Being Of Age meant much, much more than voting, Ross found out. For one thing, it meant freedom to marry—after the enforced sexlessness of the junior years and the directed breeding via artificial insemination of the Scholars. It meant a healthy head start on seniority, which carried with it all offices and all power.

It meant freedom.

As a bare beginning, it meant the freedom to command any number of juniors or scholars. On Ross's last punitive day in the dye vats, a happy ancient commandeered the entire staff to help set shrubs in his front lawn—a good dozen acres of careful landscaping it was, and the prettiest sight Ross had seen on this ugly planet.

When they got back to the dye vats, the yellow and blue had boiled over, and broken strands of yarn had fouled all the bobbins. Dobermann raged at the juniors.

But then Dobermann's raging came to an end forever. It was the night before Holiday, and there was a pretty ceremony as he packed his kit and got ready to turn Junior Unit Twenty-Three over to his successor. Everyone was scrubbed, and though a certain amount of license in regard to neatness was allowed between dinner and lights out, each bunk was made and carefully smoothed free of wrinkles. After half an hour of fidgety waiting, Dobermann called—needlessly—for attention, and the minister came in with his ancient retinue.

The rich mechanical voice boomed out from his breastplate: "Junior Dobermann, today you are a man!"

Dobermann stood with his head bowed, silent and content. Junior Twenty-Three chanted antiphonally: "Good-bye, Junior Dobermann!"

The retinue took three steps forward, and the minister boomed, "Beauty comes with age. Age is beauty!"

And the chorus: "Old heads are wisest!" Ross, standing as straight as any of them, faked the words with his lips and tongue, and wondered how many repetitions had drilled those sentiments into Junior Unit Twenty-Three.

There were five more chants, and five responses, and then the minister and his court of four were standing next to Dobermann. Breathing heavily from his exertions, the minister reached behind him and took a book from the hands of the nearest of his retinue. He said, panting, "Scholar Dobermann, in the Book lies the words of the Fathers. Read them and learn."

The chorus cried thrice, "The Word of the Fathers Is Law." And then the minister touched Dobermann's hand, and in solemn silence, left.

As soon as the elders had gone, the juniors flocked around Dobermann to wish him well. There was excited laughter in the congratulations, and a touch of apprehension too: Dobermann, with all his faults, was a known quantity, and the members of Junior Unit Twenty-Three were beginning to look a little fearfully at the short, red-headed youth who, from the next day on, would be Dobermann's successor.

Ross promised himself: He can be good or bad, a blessing or a problem. But he won't be *my* problem. I'm getting out of here tomorrow!

Holiday. "What is it, exactly?" he asked Helena.

"Oh, it's fun," Helena told him enthusiastically. "First you get up early to get the voting out of the way——"

"Voting?"

"Sure. Don't they vote where you come from? I thought everybody voted. That's democracy, like we have it here."

He sardonically quoted one of the omnipresent wall signs: "THE HAPPINESS OF THE MAJORITY MEANS THE HAPPINESS OF THE MINORITY." He had often wondered what, if anything, it meant. But Helena solemnly nodded.

They were whispering from their adjoining cots by dim, false dawn filtering through the windows on Holiday morning. They were not the only whisperers. Things were relaxing already.

"Ross," Helena said.

"Yes?"

"I thought maybe you might not know. On Holiday if you, ah, want to do that again you don't have to wait until I faint. Ah, of course you don't do it right out in the open." Overcome by her own daring she buried her head under the coarse blanket.

Fine, thought Ross wearily. Once a year—or did Holiday come once a year?—the kids were allowed to play "Spin The Bottle." No doubt their elders thought it was too cute for words: Mere tots of thirty and thirty-five childishly and innocently experimenting with sex. Of course it would be discreetly supervised so that nobody would Get In Trouble.

He was quite sure Helena's last two faints had been unconvincing phonies.

The wake-up whistle blew at last. The chattering members of Junior Unit Twenty-Three dawdled while they dressed, and the new foreman indulgently passed out shabby, smutted ribbons which the girls tied in their hair. They had sugar on their mush for breakfast, and Ross's stomach came near turning as he heard burbles of gratitude at the feast.

With pushing and a certain amount of inexpert horseplay they formed a column of fours and hiked from the hall—from the whole factory complex, indeed, along a rubberized highway.

Once you got out of the factory area things became pleasanter by the mile. Hortatory roadside signs thinned out and vanished. Stinking middens of industrial waste were left behind. And then the landscape was rolling, sodded areas with the road pleasantly springing underfoot, the air clean and crisp.

They oohed and aahed at houses glimpsed occasionally (in the distance—always) rambling, one-story affairs that looked spanking-new.

Once a car overhauled them on the highway and slowed to a crawl. It was a huge thing, richly upholstered within. A pair of grim-looking youths were respectively chauffeur and footman; the passenger waved at the troop from Junior Twenty-Three and grinned out of a fantastic landscape of wrinkles. Ross gaped. Had he thought the visiting minister was old? This creature, male or female, was *old*.

After the car sped on, to the cheers of the marchers, there was happy twittering speculation. Junior Twenty-Three didn't recognize the Citizen who had graciously waved to them, but they thought he—or she?—was wonderful. So dignified, so distinguished, so learned, so gracious, so democratic!

"Wasn't it sweet of him?" Helena burbled. "And I'm sure he must be somebody important connected with the voting, otherwise he'd just vote from home."

Ross's feet were beginning to hurt when they reached the suburban center. To the best of his recollection, they were no more than eight or ten kilometers from the field and his starship. Backtrack on the road to the surburban center about three kilometers, take the fork to the right, and that would be that.

Junior Twenty-Three reached a pitch of near-ecstasy marveling at the low, spacious buildings of the center. Through sweeping, transparent windows they saw acres of food and clothing in the shopping center; the Drive-In Theater was an architectural miracle. The Civic Center almost finished them off, with its statue of Equal Justice

Under the Law (a dignified beldame whose chin and nose almost met, leaning on a gem-crusted crutch) and Civic Virtue (in a motorized wheelchair equipped with an emergency oxygen tent, auxiliary blood pump and an artificial kidney).

Merry oldsters were everywhere in their cars and wheelchairs, gaily waving at the kids. Only one untoward incident marred their prevoting tour of inspection. A thick-headed young man mistakenly called out a cheerful: "Life and wisdom, ma'am!" to a beaming oldster.

"Ma'am, is it?" the oldster roared through his throat mike and amplifier in an unmistakable baritone. "I'll ma'am you, you wise punk!" He spun his wheelchair on a decishield, threw it into high and roared down on the offender, running him over. The boy covered himself as well as he could while the raging old man backed over him again and ran over him again. His ordeal ended when the oldster collapsed forward in the chair, hanging from his safety belt.

The boy got up with tire marks on him and groaned: "Oh, lord! I've hurt him." He appealed hysterically: "What'll I do? Is he dead?"

Another Senior Citizen buzzed up and snapped: "Cut in his heart pump, you booby!"

The boy turned on the pump, trembling. The white-faced juniors of Twenty-Three watched as the tubes to the oldster's left arm throbbed and pulsed. A massive sigh went up when the old man's eyes opened and he sat up groggily. "What happened?"

"You died again, Sherrington," said the other elder. "Third time this week—good thing there was a responsible person around. Now get over to the medical center this minute and have a complete checkup. Hear me?"

"Yes, Dad," Sherrington said weakly. He rolled off in low gear.

His father turned to the youngster who stood vacantly rubbing the tire marks on his face. "Since it's Holiday," he grated, "I'll let this pass. On any other day I would have seen to it that you were set back fifteen years for your disgraceful negligence."

Ross knew by then what that meant, and shuddered with the rest. It amounted to a death sentence, did fifteen additional years of the grinding toil and marginal diet of a junior.

Somewhat dampened they proceeded to the Hall of Democracy, a glittering place replete with slogans, statues and heroic portraits of the heroic aged. Twenty-Three huddled together as it joined with a stream of juniors from the area's other factory units. Most of them were larger than the cable works; many of them, apparently, involved more wearing and hazardous occupations. Some groups coughed incessantly and were red-eyed from the irritation of some chemical. Others must have been heavy-manual-labor specialists. They were divided into the hale, whose muscles bulged amazingly, and the dying—men and women who obviously could not take the work but who were doing it anyway.

They seated themselves at long benches, with push buttons at each station. Helena, next to him, explained the system to Ross. Voting was universal and simultaneous, in all the Halls of Democracy around the planet and from all the homes of the Senior Citizens who did not choose to vote from a Hall. Simultaneously the votes were counted at a central station and the results were flashed to screens in the Centers and homes. She said a number of enthusiastic things about Democracy while Ross studied a sheet on which the candidates and propositions were listed.

The names meant nothing to him. He noted only that each of three candidates for Chief of State was one hundred thirty years old, that each of three candidates for First Assistant Chief was one hundred and twenty-seven years old, and so on. Obviously the nominating conventions by agreement named candidates of the same age for each office to keep it a contest.

Proposition One read: "To dismantle seven pediatric centers and apply the salvage value to the construction of, and the funds no longer required for their maintenance to the maintenance of, a new wing of the Gerontological Center, said wing to be devoted to basic research in the extension of human life."

Proposition Two was worse. Proposition Two looked at first like a clear-cut boon tossed to the young, because it said that the minimum age for marriage was to be reduced from forty to thirty-two ... but then added that this would apply only if the other party to the marriage was no less than sixty. Proposition Three simply removed all restrictions on working hours for ages twenty-eight and below.

"But— But—" gasped Ross, staring at Helena, "But—"

"What's the matter, Ross?" she asked sympathetically. "Don't understand the hard words? It's all right. We don't vote on *them*. They just pass, you know, automatically if the candidate that's elected is in favor of them."

"Which candidate is in favor of them?"

"Why, they all are, of course. Now hush!" She pointed to a screen at the front of the hall. "It's starting!"

A Senior Citizen of a very high rank (his face was entirely hidden by an oxygen mask) was speaking from the screen. There was what seemed to be a ritual speech of invocation, then he got down to business. "Citizens," he said through his throat mike, "behold Democracy in Action! I give you three candidates for Chief of State—look them over, and make up your minds. First, Citizen Raphael Flexner, age one century, three decades, seven months, ten days." Senior Citizen Flexner rolled on screen, spoke briefly through his throat mike and rolled off. The first speaker said again, "Behold Democracy in Action! See now Citizen Sheridan Farnsworth, age one century, three decades, ten months, forty-two days." Applause boomed louder; some of the younger juniors yelled hysterically and drummed their heels on the floor.

Helena was panting with excitement, eyes bright on the screen. "Isn't it *wonderful*?" she gasped ecstatically. "Oh, look at *him*!"

"Him" was the third candidate, and the first oldster Ross had seen whose gocart was a wheeled stretcher. Prone and almost invisible through the clusters of tubing and chromed equipment, Senior Citizen Immanuel Appleby acknowledged his introduction—"Age one century, three decades, eleven months and five days!" The crowd went mad; Helena broke from Ross's side and joined a long yelling snake dance through the corridors.

Ross yelled experimentally as protective coloration, then found himself yelling because everybody was yelling, because he couldn't help it. By the time the speaker on the screen began to call for order, Ross was standing on top of the voting bench and screaming his head off.

Helena, weeping with excitement, tugged at his leg. "Vote now, Ross," she begged, and all over the hall the cry was "Vote! Vote!"

Ross reached out for the voting buttons. "What do we do now?" he asked Helena.

"Push the button marked 'Appleby,' of course. Hurry!"

"But why Appleby?" Ross objected. "That fellow Flexner, for instance——"

"Hush, Ross! Somebody might be listening." There was sickening fright on Helena's face. "Didn't you hear? We *have* to vote for the best man. 'Oldest is Bestest,' you know. That's what Democracy *means*, the freedom of choice. They read us the ages, and we choose which is oldest. Now please, Ross, hurry before somebody starts asking questions!"

The voting was over, and the best man had won in every case. It was a triumph for informed public opinion. The mob poured out of the hall in happy-go-lucky order, all precedences and formalities suspended for Holiday.

Helena grasped Ross firmly by the arm. The crowd was spreading over the quiet acres surrounding the Center, each little cluster heedlessly intent on a long-planned project of its own. Under the pressure of Helena's arm, Ross found himself swerving toward a clump of shrubbery.

He said violently, "No! That is, I mean I'm sorry, Helena, but I've got something to do."

She stared at him with shock in her eyes. "On Holiday?"

"On Holiday. Truly, Helena, I'm sorry. Look,

what you said last night—from now till tomorrow morning, I can do what I want, right?"

Sullenly, "Yes. I *thought*, Ross, that I *knew* what——"

"Okay." He jerked his arm away, feeling like all of the hundred possible kinds of a skunk. "See you around," he said over his shoulder. He did not look back.

Three kilometers back, he told himself firmly, then the right-hand fork in the road. And not more than a dozen kilometers, at the most, to the spaceport. He could do it in a couple of hours.

One thing had been established for certain: If ever there had been a "Franklin Foundation" on this planet, it was gone for good now. Dismantled, no doubt, to provide building materials for an eartrumpet plant. No doubt the little F-T-L ship that the Franklin Foundation was supposed to cover for was still swinging in an orbit within easy range of the spaceport; but the chance that anybody would ever find it, or use it if found, was pretty close to zero. If they bothered to maintain a radar watch at all—any other watch than the fully automatic one set to respond only to highvelocity interstellar ships—and if anyone ever took time to look at the radar plot, no doubt the F-T-L ship was charted. As an asteroid, satellite, derelict or "body of unknown origin." Certainly no one of these smug oldsters would take the trouble to investigate.

The only problem to solve on this planet was how to get off it—fast.

On the road ahead of him was what appeared to be a combination sex orgy and free-for-all. It rolled in a yelling, milling mob of half a hundred excited juniors across the road toward him, then swerved into the fields as a cluster of screaming women broke free and ran, and the rest of the crowd roared after them.

Ross quickened his step. If he ever did get off this planet, it would have to be today; he was not fool enough to think that any ordinary day would give him the freedom to poke around the spaceport's defenses. And it would be just his luck, he thought bitterly, to get involved in a gang fight on the way to the port.

There was a squeal of tires behind him, and a little vehicle screeched to a halt. Ross threw up a defensive arm in automatic reflex.

But it was only Helena, awkwardly fumbling open the door of the car. "Get in," she said sourly. "You've spoiled *my* Holiday. Might as well do what *you* want to do."

"What's that?"

Helena looked where he was pointing, and shrugged. "Guard box," she guessed. "How would I know? Nobody's in it, anyhow."

Ross nodded. They had abandoned the car and were standing outside a long, seamless fence that surrounded the spaceport. The main gates were closed and locked; a few hundred feet to the right was a smaller gate with a sort of pillbox, but that had every appearance of being locked too.

"All right," said Ross. "See that shed with the boxes outside it? Over we go."

The shed was right up against the fence; the metal boxes gave a sort of rough and just barely climbable foothold. Helena was easy enough to lift to the top of the shed; Ross, grunting, managed to clamber after her.

They looked down at the ground on the other

side, a dozen feet away. "You don't have to come along," Ross told her.

"That's just *like* you!" she flared. "Cast me aside—trample on me!"

"All right, all right." Ross looked around, but neither junior nor elder was anywhere in sight. "Hang by your hands and then drop," he advised her. "Get moving before somebody shows up."

"On Holiday?" she asked bitterly. She squirmed over the narrow top of the fence, legs dangling, let herself down as far as she could, and let go. Ross watched anxiously, but she got up quickly enough and moved to one side.

Ross plopped down next to her, knocking the wind out of himself. He got up dizzily.

His ship, in lonesome quiet, was less than a quarter of a mile away. "Let's go," Ross panted, and clutched her hand. They skirted another shed and were in the clear, running as fast as they could.

Almost in the clear.

Ross heard the whine of the little scooter before he felt the blow, but it was too late. He sprawled on the ground, dragging Helena after him.

A Senior Citizen with a long-handled rod of the sort Ross remembered all too well was scowling down at them. "Children," he rumbled through his breast-speaker in a voice of awful disgust, "is this the way to act on Holiday?"

Helena, gibbering in terror, was beyond words. Ross croaked, "Sorry, sir. We—we were just——"

Crash! The rod came down again, and every muscle in Ross's body convulsed. He rolled helplessly away, the elder following him. Crash! "We give you Holiday," the elder boomed, "and——" crash "——you act like animals. Terrible! Don't

you know that freedom of play on Holiday——"
crash "——is the most sacred right of every
junior——" crash "——and heaven help you——"
crash "——if you abuse it!"

The wrenching punishment and the caressing
voice stopped together. Ross lay blinking into the
terrible silence that followed. He became conscious
of Helena's weeping, and forced his head to turn to
look at her.

She was standing behind the elder's scooter, a
length of wire in her hand. The senior lay slumped
against his safety strap. "Ross!" she moaned. "Ross,
what have I done? *I turned him off!*"

He stood up, coughing and retching. No one else
was in sight, only the two of them and the silent,
slack form of the old man. He grabbed her arm.
"Come on," he said fuzzily, and started toward the
starship.

She hung back, mumbling to herself, her eyes
saucers. She was in a state of grievous shock, it
was clear.

Ross hesitated, rubbing his back. He knew that
she might never pull out of it. Even if she did, she
was certain to be a frightful handicap. But it was
crystal-clear that she had declared herself on his
side. Even if the elder could be revived, the punishment in store for Helena would be awful to
contemplate. . . .

Come what may, he was now responsible for
Helena.

He towed her to the starship. She climbed in
docilely enough, sat staring blankly as he sealed
ship and sent it blasting off the face of the planet.

She didn't speak until they were well into deep
space. Then the blank stare abruptly clouded and
she exploded in a fit of tears. Ross said ineffectu-

ally, "There, there." The words had no effect until
he thought to supplement them with holding her in
his arms. Then the howling in his ear subsided to
sobs and the two fugitives clung to each other without words. It was, Ross thought, kind of him to
comfort the girl when so much was on his own
mind. It was just a coincidence that he, too, found
comfort in holding her. Men comforted women;
that was how it went.

If there was anything wrong with his appraisal
of the situation, at least the error was shared.
"Thank you, Ross," Helena said hoarsely at last,
releasing him to dab at her eyes.

"Not at all," he said gruffly. He reached out to
comfort her some more, but she slipped away.

"What do I do now?" she said practically, looking around at the inside of the spaceship.

"Why, I guess you come right along with me,"
said Ross reassuringly. "There's plenty of food and
air, and plenty of room."

She peered into the other cubicle. "There isn't
plenty of room, actually," she announced. "Maybe
there's enough for a while. Where are we going?"

"Where? You mean, where?" Ross scratched his
head. "Well, let's see. Frankly, Helena, your planet
was quite a disappointment to me."

"I'm sorry, Ross," she said humbly.

"It's not your fault. You see, the thing is— Let
me begin from the beginning. On Halsey's Planet,
where I came from, things were going downhill.
Even as a young man I became aware that decay
was spreading. People seemed to be getting dumber
and dumber. Things wore out. The population was
declining. The government didn't seem even to
know what was going on, much less be able to do
anything about it—"

"Because they didn't go by seniority, right?" Helena said helpfully.

"No!" Ross roared. "*Not* because they didn't go by seniority! That's no good, either! No, the problem is a lot more fundamental than that. It has something to do with genetics. It's a matter of L-sub-T equals L-sub-zero e to the minus-T-over-two-N, if you know what I mean." She gazed at him admiringly. "And it's not just Halsey's Planet, because there are many, many worlds which have declined even farther than my planet or yours. They have dropped out of communication entirely."

She nodded. "We didn't do that," she pointed out proudly.

Ross stared at her darkly. "I'll get through this briefing a lot faster if you don't interrupt," he told her. "At any rate, I'm trying to find out what's wrong, all over the universe. And then I'm going to set it right, if I can."

She asked with interest, "How are you going to do that, Ross?" Then she dropped her eyes under his glare, and added humbly, "I mean, right now?"

"We go to the next planet, of course," he told her. "Now, please be quiet while I work this out." He turned his back on her to consult the master charts. Haarland's instructions had been to visit a place called Azor. According to the charts it was conveniently at hand, at least in the strange geodesics of the Wesley Effect, where the far galaxies might be close nearby in the warped space-lines, while the void just beyond the viewplates might be infinitely distant. "The F-T-L family on Azor was named Cavallo when they were last heard from," he announced. "They were builders of machine tools. That's good. That's technology. They'll have to have kept some kind of scientific training going for that, and—"

"Ross?" she offered diffidently.

"Please! And that means that they'll be at least open-minded when I talk to them. Probably they'll have come to the same conclusions themselves. Probably they might even have started their own program of research and exploration—oh, what is it now?"

"Just that if we're going somewhere I think we'd better go," she said, waving to the viewplates, "because it looks to me like the planet's been getting a lot bigger. Could we be falling back?"

Cursing, Ross sprang to the huge board and began setting up the F-T-L problem, one eye over his shoulder on the rapidly growing disk of Helena's planet. He reached a solution just as the first whistle of atmosphere told him they were getting dangerously close, and then the Wesley Drive cut in and they were on their way.

7

They were well within detection range of Azor's radar, if any, and yet there had been no beeping signal that the planet's GCA had taken over and would pilot them down. Had they drawn another blank? He studied the surface of the world under his highest magnification and saw no signs that it had been devastated by war. There were cities—intact, as far as he could tell, though not very attractive. The design ran to huge, gloomy piles that mounted toward central towers.

Azor was a big world which showed not much water and a great deal of black rock. It was the fifth of its system and reportedly had colonized its four adjacent neighbors and their moons.

His own search radar pinged. The signal was followed at once by a guarded voice from his ship-to-ship communicator: "What ship are you? Do you receive me? The band is 798.44."

Ross hastily dialed the frequency on his transmitter and called, "I receive you. We are a vessel from outside your solar system, home planet Halsey. We want to contact a family named Cavallo of the planet Azor believed to be engaged in building machine tools. Can you help us?"

There was a pause. "Are you a male?"

"Of course I'm a male!" Ross barked. "I'm a male from Halsey's Planet, a good many light-years away."

There was an even longer pause. The voice asked cautiously, "Are you, uh, in command? Or just the communicator, like me?"

"I'm the captain," Ross roared, glaring at Helena, who gazed back uncomprehendingly. She opened her mouth to ask a question, but Ross froze her with a frown. "What I want from you," he explained to the unseen communicator, "is advice on how to contact your landing grid and nothing else."

"You don't have to worry about that," sighed the voice, "because they'll contact you soon enough. But if you want advice I'll give it. Sheer off this system, my friend. Go somewhere else."

"What is this? Who are you?"

"My name does not matter. I happen to be on watch aboard the prison orbital station *Minerva*. Get going, my friend, before the planetary GCA picks you up."

Prison orbital station? A very sensible idea. "Thanks for the advice," he parried. "Can you tell me anything about the Cavallo family?"

"I have heard of them. My friend, your time is running out. If you do not sheer off very soon they will land you. And I judge from the tone of your voice that it will not be long before you join the rest of us criminals aboard *Minerva*. It is not pleasant here. Good-by."

"Wait, please!" Ross had no intention at all of committing any crimes that would land him aboard a prison hulk, and he had every intention of fulfilling his mission. "Tell me about the Cavallo family—and why you expect me to get in trouble on Azor."

"The time is running out, my friend, but—the Cavallo family of machine tool builders is located in Novj Grad. And the crime of which all of us aboard *Minerva* were convicted is conspiracy to advocate equality of the sexes. Now go!"

The carrier-wave hum of the communicator died. Ross tapped his teeth irresolutely. "I wonder," he said, "if we aren't making some kind of mistake, landing here."

"But that couldn't be," Helena said helpfully, "because this is the planet you're supposed to go to, right?"

"But things change," he complained. "I don't know. Maybe we ought to vector in on that satellite." He gestured at the board. "All it would take would be one command, lock and dock."

"But why would we want to go to a prison satellite, Ross?"

"For information," he snarled. "Didn't you hear all that? That man was trying to tell me something! And it didn't sound good."

But how it sounded no longer mattered, for another electronic noise filled the cabin—the beep of a GCA radar taking over the sealed landing controls of the craft.

"Well, we'll find everything out in a minute," Helena said brightly. "I wouldn't worry about that person. He sounded very young, if you know what I mean, and besides what was he doing on a prison satellite if he wasn't some kind of prisoner himself?"

The ship began to jet tentative bursts of reaction mass, nosing toward the big, gloomy planet.

"He called me his friend," Ross mused, "and I think he meant it. We could be in big trouble here, Helena."

"Oh, I don't think so, Ross," she objected. "I mean, home is a long way away. There isn't any way they could, uh, know about us? I mean about, you know, the disconnection? The Senior Citizens here won't know about the Senior Citizens there, will they?"

He tried to break it to her gently as the ship picked up speed. "Helena, it's possible that the old people here won't be Senior Citizens—not in your planet's sense. They may just be old people. I think, in fact, that we may find you outranking older people who happen to be males."

She took it as a joke. "You are funny, Ross. Old means Senior, doesn't it? And Senior means better, wiser, abler, and in charge, doesn't it?"

"We'll see," he said thoughtfully as the main reaction drive cut in. "We'll see very shortly."

The spaceport was bustling, busy, and efficient. Ross marveled at the speed and dexterity with which the anonymous ground operator whipped his ship into a braking orbit and set it down. And he stared enviously at the crawling clamshells on treads, bigger than houses, that cupped around his ship; the ship was completely and hermetically surrounded, and bathed in a mist of germicides and prophylactic rays.

A helmeted figure riding a little platform on the inside of one of the clamshells turned a series of knobs, climbed down, and rapped on the ship's entrance port.

Ross opened it diffidently, and almost strangled in the antiseptic fumes. Helena choked and wheezed behind him as the figure threw back its helmet and said, "Where's the captain?"

"I am he," said Ross meticulously. "I would like to be put in touch with the Cavallo Machine Tool Company of Novj Grad."

The figure shook its long hair loose, which provided Ross with the necessary clue: It was a woman. Not a very attractive-looking woman, for she wore no makeup; but by the hair, by the brows and by the smoothness of her chin, a woman all the same. She said coldly, "If you're the captain, who's that?"

Helena said in a small voice, "I'm Helena, from Junior Unit Twenty-Three."

"Indeed." Suddenly the woman smiled. "Well, come ashore, dear," she said. "You must be tired from your trip. Both of you come ashore," she added graciously.

She led the way out of the clamshells to a waiting closed car. Azor's sun had an unpleasant bluish cast to it, not a type-G at all; Ross thought that the lighting made the woman look uglier than she really had to be. Even Helena looked pinched and bloodless, which he knew well was not the case at all.

All around them was activity. Whatever this planet's faults, it was not a stagnant home for graybeards. Ross, craning, saw nothing that was shoddy, nothing that would have looked out of place in the best-equipped port of Halsey's Planet. And the reception lounge, or whatever it was, that the woman took them to was a handsome and prettily furnished construction. "Some lunch?" the woman asked, directing her attention to Helena. "A cup of tribrew, maybe? Let me have the boy bring some."

Helena looked to Ross for signals, and Ross, gritting his teeth, nodded to her to agree. Too young the last time, too male this time; was there ever going to be a planet where he mattered to anyone?

He said desperately, "Madam, forgive my interruption, but this lady and myself need urgently to get in touch with the Cavallo company. Is this Novj Grad?"

The woman's pale brows arched. She said, with an effort, "No, it is not."

"Then can you tell us where Novj Grad is?" Ross persisted. "If they have a spaceport, we can hop over there in our ship——"

The woman gasped something that sounded like, "Well!" She stood up and said pointedly to Helena, "If you'll excuse me, I have something to attend to." And swept out.

Helena stared wide-eyed at Ross. "She must've been a real Senior Citizen, huh?"

"Not exactly," said Ross despairingly. "Look, Helena, things are different here. I need your help."

"Help?"

"Yes, help!" he bellowed. "Get a grip on yourself, girl. Remember what I told you about the planet I came from? It was different from yours, remember? The old people were just like anybody else." She giggled in embarrassment. "They were!" he yelled. "And they are here, too. Old people, young people, doesn't matter. On my planet, the richest people were—well, never mind. On this planet, women are the bosses. Get it? Wome are like the elders. So you'll have to take over, Helena."

She was looking at him with a puzzled frown. She objected, "But if women are——"

"They are. Never mind about that part of it now; just remember that for the purposes of getting along here, you're going to be my boss. You tell me what to do. You talk to everybody. And what you have to say to them is this: You must get to Novj Grad immediately, and talk to a high-ranking member of the Cavallo MachineTool Company. Clear? Once we get there, I'll take over; everything will be under control then." He added prayerfully, "I hope."

Helena blinked at him. "I'm going to be your boss?" she asked.

"That's right."

"Like an elder bosses a junior? And it's legal?"

Ross started to repeat, "That's right," impatiently again. But there was a peculiar look in Helena's round eyes. "Helena!" he said warningly.

She was all concern. "Why, what is it, Ross?" she asked solicitously. "You look upset. Just leave everything to me, dear."

They got started on the way to Novj Grad—not in their ship (the woman had said there was no spaceport in Novj Grad), and not alone, so that Ross could not confirm his unhappy opinion of Helena's inner thoughts. But at least they were on their way to Novj Grad in the Azorian equivalent of a chartered aircraft, with Helena chatting happily with the female pilot, and Ross sitting uncomfortably on a narrow, upholstered strip behind.

Everything he saw in Azor confirmed his first impressions. The planet was busy and prosperous. Nobody seemed to be doing anything very productive, he thought, but somehow everything seemed to get done. Automatic machinery, he guessed; if women were to have any chance of gaining the upper hand on a planet, most of the hard physical work would have to be fairly well mechanized anyhow. And particularly on this planet. They had been flying for six hours, at a speed he guessed to be not much below that of sound, and fully half of the territory they passed over was bare, black rock.

The ship began losing altitude, and the pilot, who had been curled up in a relaxed position, totally ignoring the aircraft, glanced at her instrument panel. "Coming in for a landing," she warned. "Don't distract me right now, dear, I've got a thousand things to do."

She didn't seem to be doing any of them, Ross thought disapprovingly; all she did was watch varicolored lights blink on and off. But no doubt the ship landing, too, was as automatic as the piloting.

Helena turned and leaned back to Ross. "We're coming in for a landing," she relayed.

Ross said sourly, "I heard."

Helena gave him a look of reprimand and forgiveness. "I'm hungry," she mused.

The pilot turned from her controls. "You can get something at the airport," she offered eagerly. "I'll show you."

Helena looked at Ross. "Would you like something?"

But the pilot frowned. "I don't believe there's any place for men," she said disapprovingly. "Perhaps we can get something sent out for him if you like. Although, really, it's probably against the rules, you know."

Ross started to say with great dignity, "Thank you, but that won't be necessary." But he didn't quite get it out. The ship came in for its landing. There was an enormous jolt and a squawk of alarm bells and flashing lights. The ship careened crazily, and stopped.

"Oh, darn," complained the pilot mildly. "It's

always doing that. Come on, dear, let's get something to eat. We'll come back for *him* later."

And Ross was left alone to stare apprehensively at the unceasingly flashing lights and to listen to the strident alarms for three-quarters of an hour.

His luck was in, though. The ship didn't explode. And eventually a pallid young man in a greasy apron appeared with a tray of sandwiches and a vacuum jug, looking around nervously.

"Up here, boy," Ross called.

The youth gaped through the port. "You mean come in?"

"Sure. It's all right."

The young man put down the tray. Something in the way he looked at it prompted Ross to invite him: "Have some with me? More here than I can handle."

"Thanks; I believe I will. I, uh, was supposed to take my break after I brought you this stuff." He poured steaming brew into the cup that covered the jug, politely pushed it to Ross and swigged from the jug himself. "You're with the starship?" he asked, around a mouthful of sandwich.

"Yes. I—the captain, that is—wants to contact an outfit called Cavallo Machine Tool. You know where they are?"

"Sure. Biggest firm on the south side. Fifteen Street; you can't miss them. The captain—is she the lady who was with Pilot Breuer?"

"Yes."

The youngster's eyes widened. "You mean you were in space—alone—with a lady?"

Ross nodded and chewed.

"And she didn't—uh—there wasn't—well—any problem?"

"No," said Ross. "You have much trouble with that kind of thing?"

The boy winced. "If I've asked once I've asked a hundred times for a transfer. Oh, those jet pilots! I used to work in a roadside truck stop. I know truckers are supposed to be rough and tough; maybe they are. But you can't tell me that deep down a trucker isn't a lady. When you tell them no, that's that. But a pilot—it just eggs them on. Azor City today, Novj Grad tomorrow—what do they care?"

Ross was fascinated and baffled. It seemed to him that they should care and care plenty. Back where he came from, it was the woman who paid and he couldn't imagine any cultural setup which could alter that biological fact. He asked cautiously: "Have you ever been—in trouble?"

The boy stiffened and looked disapproving. Then he said with a sigh: "I might as well tell you. It's all over the station anyway; they call me 'Bernie the Pullover.' Yes. Twice. Pilots both times. I can't seem to say no——" He took aother long pull from the jug and a savage bite from a second sandwich.

"I'm sure," Ross said numbly, "it wasn't your fault."

"Try telling that to the judge," Bernie the Pullover said bitterly. "The pilot speaks her piece, the medic puts the blood group tests in evidence, the doctor and crèche director depose that the child was born and is still living. Then the judge says, without even looking up, 'Paternity judgment to the plaintiff, defendant ordered to pay one thousand credits annual support, let this be a warning to you, young man, next case.' I shouldn't have joined you and eaten your sandwiches, but the fact is I was hungry. I had to sell my meal voucher yesterday to meet my payment. Miss three payments and——" He jerked his thumb heavenward.

Ross thought and realized that the thumb must indicate the orbiting prison hulk *Minerva*. It *was* the man who paid here.

He demanded: "How did all this happen?"

Bernie, having admitted his hunger, had stopped stalling and seized a third sandwich. "All what?" he asked indistinctly.

Ross thought hard and long. He realized first that he could probably never explain what he meant to Bernie, and second that if he did they'd probably both wind up aboard *Minerva* for conspiracy to advocate equality. He shifted his ground. "Of course everybody agrees on the natural superiority of women," he said, "but people seem to differ from planet to planet as to the reasons. What do they say here on Azor?"

"Oh—nothing special or fancy. Just the common-sense, logical thing. They're smaller, for one thing, and haven't got the muscles of men, so they're natural supervisors. They accumulate money as a matter of course because men die younger and women are the beneficiaries. Then, women have a natural aptitude for all the interesting jobs. I saw a broadcast about that just the other night. The biggest specialist on the planet in vocational aptitude. I forgot her name, but she proved it conclusively."

He looked at the empty platter before them. "I've got to go now. Thanks for everything."

"The pleasure was mine." Ross watched his undernourished figure head for the station. He swore a little, and then buckled down to some hard thinking. Helena was his key to this world. He'd have to have a long skull-session or two with her; he couldn't be constantly prompting her or there would be serious trouble. She would be the front and he would be the very inconspicuous brains of the outfit, trailing humbly behind. But was she capable of absorbing a brand-new, rather complicated concept? She seemed to be, he told himself uncomfortably, in love with him. That would help considerably. . . .

Helena and Pilot Breuer showed up, walking with a languor that suggested a large and pleasant meal disposed of. Helena's first words disposed with shocking speed of Ross's doubts that she was able to acquire a brand-new sociological concept. They were: "Ah, there you are, my dear. Did the boy bring you something or other to eat?"

"Yes. Thanks. Very thoughtful of you," he said pointedly, with one eye on Breuer's reaction. There was none; he seemed to have struck the right note.

"Pilot Breuer," said Helena blandly, "thinks I'd enjoy an evening doing the town with her and a few friends."

"But the Cavallo people——"

"Ross," she said gently, "don't *nag*."

He shut up. And thought: wait until I get her out into space. *If* I get her out into space. She'd be a damned fool to leave this wacked-up culture. . . .

Breuer was saying, with an altogether too-innocent air, "I'd better get you two settled in a hotel for the night; then I'll pick up Helena and a few friends and we'll show her what old Novj Grad has to offer in the way of night life. Can't have her batting around the universe saying Azor's sidewalks are rolled up at 2100, can we? And then she can do her trading or whatever it is with Cavallo bright and early tomorrow, eh?"

Ross realized that he was being jollied out of an attack of the sulks. He didn't like it.

*   *   *

The hotel was small and comfortable, with a bar crowded by roistering pilots and their dates. The glimpses Ross got of social life on Azor added up to a damnably unfair picture. It was the man who paid. Breuer roguishly tested the mattress in their room, nudging Helena, and then announced, "Get settled, kids, while I visit the bar."

When the door rolled shut behind her Ross said furiously: "Look, you! Protective mimicry's fine up to a point, but let's not forget what this mission is all about. We seem to be suckered into spending the night, but by hell tomorrow morning bright and early we find those Cavallo people—"

"There," Helena said soothingly. "Don't be angry, Ross. I promise I won't be out late, and she really did insist."

"I suppose so," he grumbled. "Just remember it's no pleasure trip."

"Not for you, perhaps," she smiled sweetly.

He let it drop there, afraid to push the matter.

Breuer returned in about ten minutes with a slight glow on. "It's all fixed," she told Helena. "Got a swell crowd lined up. Table at Virgin Willie's—oops!" She glanced at Ross. "No harm in it, of course," she said. "Anything you want, Ross, just dial service. It's on my account. I fixed it with the desk."

"Thanks."

They left, and Ross went grumpily to bed.

A secretive rustle in the room awoke him. "Helena?" he asked drowsily.

Pilot Breuer's voice giggled drunkenly, "Nope. Helena's passed out at Virgin Willie's, kind of the way I figured she would be on triple antigravs.

Had my eye on you since Azor City, baby. You gonna be nice to me?"

"Get out of here!" Ross hissed furiously. "Out of here or I'll yell like hell."

"So yell," she giggled. "I got the house dick fixed. They know me here, baby——"

He fumbled for the bedside light and snapped it on. "I'll pitch you right through the door," he announced. "And if you give me any more lip I won't bother to open it before I do."

She hiccupped and said, "A spirited lad. That's the way I like 'em." With one hand she drew a nasty-looking little pistol. With the other she pulled a long zipper and stepped out of her pilot's coveralls.

Ross gulped. There were three ways to play this, the smart way, the stupid way, and the way that all of a sudden began to look attractive. He tried the stupid way.

He got the pistol barrel alongside his ear for his pains. "Don't jump me," Pilot Breuer giggled. "The boys that've tried to take this gun away from me are stretched end to end from here to Azor City. By me, baby."

Ross blinked through a red-spotted haze. He took a deep breath and got smart. "You're pretty tough," he said admiringly.

"Oh, sure." She kicked the coveralls across the room and moved in on him. "Baby," she said caressingly, "if I seem to sort of forget myself in the next couple of minutes, don't get any ideas. I *never* let go of my gun. Move over."

"Sure," Ross said hollowly. This, he told himself disgustedly, was the damnedest, silliest, ridiculousest . . .

There was a furious hiccup from the door. "So!"

Helena said venomously, pushing the door wide and almost falling to the floor. "So!"

Ross flailed out of the bed, kicking the pistol out of Pilot Breuer's hand in the process. He cried enthusiastically, "Helena, dear!"

"Don't you 'Helena-dear' me!" she said, moving in and kicking the door shut behind her. "I leave you alone for one little minute, and what happens? And *you!*"

"Sorry," Pilot Breuer muttered, climbing into her coveralls. "Wrong room. Must've had one antigrav too many." She licked her lips apprehensively, zipping her coveralls and sidling toward the door. With one hand on the knob, she said diffidently, "If I could have my gun back——? No, you're right! I'll get it tomorrow." She got through the door just ahead of a lamp.

"Hussy!" spat Helena. "And you, Ross—"

It was the last straw. Ross lurched toward her.

Pilot Breuer had been right. Nobody paid any attention to the noise.

"Yes, Ross." Helena had hardly touched her breakfast; she sat with her eyes downcast.

" 'Yes, Ross'," he mimicked bitterly. "It better be 'Yes, Ross.' This place may look all right to you, but it's trouble. You don't want to find yourself stuck here all your life, do you? Then do what I tell you."

"Yes, Ross."

He pushed the remains of his food away. "Oh, the hell with it," he said dispiritedly. "I wish I'd never started out on this fool's errand. And I double damn well wish I'd left you in the dye vats."

"Yes, Ro—— I mean, I'm glad you didn't, Ross," she said in a small voice.

He stood up and patted her shoulder absently. "Come on," he said, "we've got to get over to the Cavallo place. I wish you had let me talk to them on the phone."

She said reasonably, "But you said——"

"I know what I said. When we get there, remember that I do the talking."

They walked through green-lit streets, filled with proud-looking women and sad-eyed men. The Cavallo Machine-Tool Corporation was only a few intersections away, by the map the desk clerk had drawn for Helena; they found it without trouble. It was a smallish sort of building for a factory, Ross thought, but perhaps that was how factories went on Azor. Besides, it was well constructed and beautifully landscaped with the purplish lawns these people seemed to prefer.

Helena led him through the door, as was right and proper. She said to the busy little bald-headed man who seemed to be the receptionist, "We're expected. Miss Cavallo, please."

"Certainly, Ma'am," he said with a gap-toothed smile, and worked a combination of rods and buttons on the desk beside him. In a moment, he said, "Go right in. Three up and four over; can't miss it."

They passed through a noisy territory of machines where metal was sliced, spun, hacked, and planed; no one seemed to be paying any attention to them. Ross wondered who had built the machines, and whether those builders were now on *Minerva*, staring at the unattainable free sky.

Miss Cavallo was a motherly type with a large black cigar. "Sit right down," she said heartily. "You, too, young man. Tell me what we in Cavallo Company can do for you."

Helena opened her mouth, but Ross stopped her with a gesture. "That's enough," he said quietly. "I'll take over. Miss Cavallo," he declaimed from memory, "what follows is under the seal."

"Is it indeed! What do you know," she said.

Ross said, "Wesley."

Miss Cavallo slapped her thigh. "Son of a gun," she said admiringly. "How this takes me back—those long-ago childhood days, learning these things at my mother's knee. Let's see. Uh—the limiting velocity is C."

"But C^2 is not a velocity," Ross finished triumphantly. And, from the heart, "Miss Cavallo, you don't begin to know how happy this makes me."

Miss Cavallo reached over and pumped his hand, then Helena's. To the girl she said, "You've got a right to be a proud woman, believe me. The way he got through it, without a single stumble! Never saw anything like it in my life. Well, just tell me what I can do for you, now that that's over."

Ross took a deep, deep breath. He said earnestly, "A great deal. I don't know where to begin. You see, it all goes back to Halsey's Planet, where I come from. This, uh, this ship came in, a longliner, and it got some of us a little worried because, well, it seemed that some of the planets were no longer in communication. We—uh, Miss Cavallo?" She was smiling pleasantly enough, but Ross had the crazy feeling that he just wasn't getting through to her.

"Go right ahead," she boomed. "God knows, I've got nothing against men in business; that's old-fashioned prejudice, mostly. Take your time. I won't bite you. Get on with your proposition, young man."

"It isn't exactly a proposition," Ross said weakly. All of a sudden the words seemed hard to find. What did you say to a potential partner in the salvation of the human race when she just nodded and blew cigar smoke at you?

He made an effort. "Halsey's Planet was the seventh alternate destination for this ship, and so we figured—— That is, Miss Cavallo, it kind of looked like there was some sort of trouble. So Mr. Haarland—he's the one who has the F-T-L secret on Halsey, like you do here on Azor—he passed it on to me, of course—well, he asked me to, well, sort of take a look around." He stopped. The words by then were just barely audible anyhow; and Miss Cavallo had been looking furtively at her watch.

Miss Cavallo shrugged sympathetically to Helena. "They're all like that under the skin, aren't they?" she observed ambiguously. "Well, if men could take our jobs away from us, what would we do? Stay home and mind the kids?" She roared and poked a box of cigars at Helena.

"Now," she said briskly, "let's get down to cases. I really enjoyed hearing those lines from you, young man, and I want you to know that I'm prepared to help you in any possible way because of them. Open a line of credit, speed up deliveries, send along some of our technical people to help you get set up—anything. Now, what can I do for you? Turret lathes? Grinders? Screw machines?"

"Miss Cavallo," Ross said desperately, "don't you know anything about the faster-than-light secret?"

She said impatiently, "Of course I do, young man. Said the responses, didn't I? There's no call for that item, though."

"I don't want to *buy* one," Ross cried. "I have one. Don't you realize that the human race is in danger? Populations are dying out or going out of communication all over the galaxy. Don't you want to do something about it before we all go under?"

Miss Cavallo dropped all traces of a smile. Her face was like flint as she stood up and pointed to the window. "Young man," she said icily, "take a look out there. That's the Cavallo Machine-Tool Company. Does that look as if we're going under?"

"I know, but Clyde, Cyrnus One, Ragansworld—at least a dozen planets I can name—are *gone*. Didn't you ever think that you might be next?"

Miss Cavallo kept her voice level, but only with a visible effort.

She said flatly, "No. Never. Young man, I have plenty to do right here on Azor without bothering my head about those places you're talking about. Seventy-five years ago there was another fellow just like you; Flarney, some name like that; my grandmother told me about him. He came bustling in here causing trouble, with that old silly jingle about Wesley and C-square and so on, with some cock-and-bull story about a planet that was starving to death, stirring up a lot of commotion. Well, he wound up on *Minerva*, because he wouldn't take no for an answer. Watch out that you don't do the same."

She marched majestically to the door. "And now," she said, "if you've wasted quite enough of my time, kindly leave."

8

"Where shall we go now, Ross?" Helena asked politely. They were walking aimlessly down Fifteen Street, the nicely landscaped machine-tool works behind them. He scowled absently at her, then turned his scowl at a plump woman in a violet jogging suit as she pumped past.

"If I knew," he said, "I'd tell you in a minute. Have you got any money left?"

"Well, not exactly," she explained. "Those drinks cost so much in that awful place! And I did have to buy a round now and then, so the money Pilot Breuer loaned me really didn't last.... Miss Cavallo didn't turn out the way you expected, did she?" she added, hastily changing the subject.

"Stupid old bat," Ross muttered. No help from Cavallo. No money. No good ideas.

Helena said timidly: "You really shouldn't talk that way, Ross. She *is* older than you, after all. Old heads are——"

"——wisest," he wearily agreed. "Also the most

conservative. Also the most rigidly inflexible; also the most firmly closed to the reception of new ideas. With one exception."

She reeled under the triple blasphemy and then faintly asked: "What's the exception?"

Ross became aware that they were not alone. Their very manner of walking, he a little ahead, obviously leading the way, was drawing unfavorable attention from passers-by. Nothing organized or even definite—just looks ranging from puzzled distaste to anger. He said, "Somebody named Haarland. Never mind," and in a lower voice: "Straighten up. Step out a little ahead of me. Scowl."

She managed it all except the scowl. The expression on her face got some stupefied looks from other pedestrians, but nothing worse.

Helena said loudly and plaintively: "I don't like it here after all, Ross. These women are so *bossy*. Even the young ones—don't they have any *manners*?"

"Watch it," Ross groaned, but he was too late.

Should the impulse seize you, placard Halsey's Planet with signs announcing trader status privileges to be an outmoded barbarism from a degenerate past. Mount a detergent box and inform a crowd of Altarians that they are degenerate slith-fondlers if you must. Announce in a crowded Cephean bar room that Sadkia Revall is no better than she should be. From these situations you have some chance of emerging intact. But never, never pronounce the word "women" as Helena pronounced it on Fifteen Street, Novj Grad, Azor.

The mob took only seconds to form.

Ross and Helena found themselves with their backs to the glass doors of a food store. The handful of women who had actually heard the remark were all talking to them simultaneously, with fist-shaking. Behind them stood as many as a dozen women who knew only that something had happened and that there were comfortably outnumbered victims available. The noise was deafening, and Helena began to cry. Ross first wondered if he could bring himself to knock down a woman; then realized after studying the hulking virago in their foreground that he might bring himself to try but probably would not succeed.

She seemed to be accusing Helena of masquerading, of advocating equality, of uttering obscenely antisocial statements in the public road, to the affront of all decent-minded girls.

There was violence in the air. Ross was on the point of blocking a roundhouse right when the glass doors opened behind them. The small diversion distracted the imbecile collective brain of the mob.

"What's going on here?" a suety voice demanded. "Ladies, may I please get through?"

It was a man trying to emerge from the food shop with a double armful of cartons. He was a great fat slob, quite hairless, and smelling powerfully of kitchen. He wore the gravy-spotted whites of any cook anywhere.

The virago said to him, "Keep out of this, Willie. This fellow here's a masquerader. The thing I heard him say——!"

"I'm not," Helena wept. "I'm not!"

The cook stooped to look into her face and turned on the mob. "She isn't," he said definitely. "She's a lady from some foreign place. She was slopping up triple antigravs at my place last night with a gang of jet pilots."

"That doesn't prove a thing!" the virago yelled.

"Madam," the cook said wearily, "after her third antigrav I had to trip her up and crown her. She was about to climb the bar and corner my barman."

Ross looked at her fixedly. She stopped crying and nervously cleared her throat.

"So if you'll just let us through," the cook bustled, seizing the psychological moment of doubt. His enormous belly bulldozed a lane for them. "Beg pardon. Excuse us. Madam, will you—thank you. Beg pardon——"

The lynchers were beginning to drift away, embarrassed. The party had collapsed. "Faster," the cook hissed at them. "Beg pardon—" And they were in the clear and well down the street.

"Thank you, Sir," Helena said humbly.

"Just 'Willie', *if* you please," the fat man said.

One hand descended on Ross's shoulder and another on Helena's. They both belonged to the virago. She spun them around, glaring. "*I'm* not satisfied with the brush-off," she snapped. "Exactly what did you mean by that remark you made?"

Helena wailed, "It's just that you and all these other women here seem so *young*."

The virago's granite face softened. She let go and tucked in a strand of steel-wool hair. "Did you really think so, dear?" she asked, beaming. "There, I'm sorry I got excited. A wee bit jealous, were you? Well, we're broad-minded here in Novj Grad." She patted Helena's arm and walked off, smiling and jaunty.

Virgin Willie led off and they followed him. Ross's knees were shaky. If that woman had had any idea what "young" meant in Helena's vocabulary—

He opened his mouth, but the cook shook him off. "Not yet!" he muttered, brightly acknowledging winks and knowing smiles from the women they passed as he walked. Obviously he was a tolerated character, for a male. One could learn from this pig, Ross thought with distaste. One could acquire the survival skills that let him move about freely in this hag-ridden world, while pursuing in some way the quest for knowledge that had brought one here. . . .

Better still, one could find a way back to one's spaceship and get one's tail as far from here as possible, and as fast.

They stopped at an alleyway. The cook looked around and said righteously, "Begging your pardon, ma'am, but that was a silly damn stunt."

"Oh, I know," Helena said apologetically. "I must have had more to drink than—"

"I'm not talking about last night, ma'am, I'm talking about *now*. Do you want to get your boyfriend an egalitarianism rap? There's been too much of that already! Everybody's nerves are absolutely ragged. If somebody gets smashed up in traffic, they blame it on us. Don't care *where* you're from. Watch it next time."

"We will, Willie," Helena said contritely. "And I think you run an awfully nice restaurant."

"Yeah," said Ross, looking at her.

Willie muttered, "I guess you're clear. You still staying at that hot pilot's hangout? This is where we say good-by, then. You turn left."

He waddled on down the street. Helena said instantly, "I don't remember a thing, Ross."

"Okay," he said. "You don't remember a thing."

She looked relieved and said brightly, "So let's get back to the hotel."

"Okay," he said. Climbed the bar and tried to corner the . . . Halfway to the hotel he slowed, then stopped, and said, "I just thought of something. Maybe we're not staying there any more. After last night why should Breuer carry us on her tab? I thought we'd have some money to carry us from the Cavallos by now——"

"The ship?" she asked in a small voice.

"Across the continent. Hell! Maybe Breuer forgave and forgot. Let's try, anyway."

They never got as far as the hotel. When they reached the square it stood on, there was a breathless rush and Bernie stood before them, panting and holding a hand over his chest. "In here," he gasped, and nodded at a shopfront that announced hot brew. Ross thoughtlessly started first through the door and caught Bernie's look of alarm. He opened the door for Helena, who went through smiling nervously.

They settled at a small table in an empty corner in stiff silence. "I've been walking around that square all morning," Bernie said, with a cowed look at Helena.

Ross told her: "This young man and I had a talk yesterday at the plane while you were eating. What is it, Bernie?"

He still couldn't believe that he was doing it, but Bernie said in a scared whisper: "Wanted to head you off and warn you. Breuer was down at the field cafe this morning, talking loud to the other hot-shots. She said you—both of you—talked equality. Said she got up with a hangover and you were gone. But she said there'd be six policewomen waiting in your room when you got back." He leaned forward on the table. Ross remembered that he had been forced to sell his ration card.

"Here comes the waiter," he said softly. "Order

something for all of us. We have a little money. And thanks, Bernie."

Helena asked, "What do we *do*?"

"We eat," Ross said practically. "Then we think. Shut up; let Bernie order."

They ate; and then they thought. Nothing much seemed to come from all the thinking, though.

They were a long, long way from the spaceship. Ross commandeered all of Helena's leftover cash. It was almost, not quite, enough for one person to get halfway back to Azor City. He and Bernie turned out their pockets and added everything they had, including pawnable valuables. That helped, a little.

Ross said, "Bernie, what would happen if we, well, stole something?"

Bernie shrugged. "It's against the law, of course. They probably wouldn't prosecute, though."

"They wouldn't?"

"Not if they can prove egalitarianism on you. Stealing's against the law; preaching equality is against the *state*. You get the maximum penalty for that."

Helena choked on her drink, but Ross merely nodded. "So we might as well take a chance," he said. "Thanks, Bernie. We won't bother you any more. You'll forget you heard this, won't you?"

"The hell I will!" Bernie squawked. "If you're getting out of here, I want to go with you! You aren't leaving *me* behind!"

"But Bernie——" Ross started. He was interrupted by the manager, a battleship-class female with a mighty prow, who came scowling toward them.

"Pipe down," she ordered coarsely. "This place

is for decent people; we don't want no distur-
bances here. If you can't act decent, get out."

"Awk," said Helena as Ross kicked her under
the table. "I mean, yes ma'am. Sorry if we were
talking too loud." They watched the manager walk
away in silence.

As soon as she was fairly away, Ross hissed, "It's
out of the question, Bernie. You might be jumping
from the frying-pan into the fire."

Bernie asked, startled, "The what?"

"The—never mind, it's just an expression where
I come from. It means you might get out of this place
and find yourself somewhere worse. We don't know
where we're going next; you might wish to God
you were back here within the next three days."

"I'll take that chance," Bernie said earnestly.
"Look, Ross, I played square with you. I didn't
have to stick my neck out and warn you. How
about giving me a break too?"

Helena interrupted, "He's right, Ross. After all,
we owe him that much, don't we? I mean, if a
person does that much for a person, a person ought
to——"

"Oh, shut up." Ross glared at both of them.
"You two seem to think this is a game," he said
bitterly. "Let me set you straight, both of you. It
isn't. More hangs on what happens to me than
either of you realize. The fate of the human race,
for instance."

Helena flashed a look at Bernie. "Of *course*, Ross,"
she said soothingly. "Both of us know that, don't
we, Bernie?"

Bernie stammered, "Sure—sure we do, Ross."
He rubbed his ankle. He went on, "Honest, Ross, I
want to get the hell away from Azor once and for
all. I don't care *where* you're going. Anything would

be better than this place and all these damned
female bloodsuckers! Call me an egalitarianist if
you want to. I don't care! All I care is that these
women are making this whole planet a living—"

He stopped, petrified. His eyes, looking over
Ross's shoulder, were enormous.

"Go on, sonny," snarled a rich female voice from
behind Ross. "Don't let me and the lieutenant stop
you just when you're going good."

"I knew I shouldn't have trusted that damn manager," Bernie said for the twentieth time. "What'd
she care about us? Worried about her license, that's
all, so she called the cops!"

Ross uncrossed his legs painfully and tried lying
on the floor on his side. "What's the difference?"
he asked. "They got us; we're in the jug. And face
it: somebody would have caught us sooner or later,
and we might have wound up in a worse jail than
this one." He shifted uncomfortably. "If that's possible, I mean. Why don't they at least have beds in
these places?"

"Oh," said Bernie immediately, "some do. The
jails in Azor City and Nuevo Reykjavik have beds;
Novj Grad, Eleanor, and Milo don't. I mean, that's
what they tell me," he added virtuously.

"Sure," Ross growled. "Well, what do they tell
you usually happens next?"

Bernie spread his hands. "Different things. First
there's a hearing. That's all over by now. Then an
indictment and trial. Maybe that's started already;
sometimes they get it in on the same day as the
hearing, sometimes not. Then—tomorrow sometime, most likely—comes the sentencing. We'll know
about that, though, because we'll be there. The

law's very strict on that—they always have you in the court for sentencing."

Ross cried, "You mean the trial might be going on right now without us?"

"Of course. What else? Think they'd take a chance on having the prisoners creating a disturbance during the trial?"

Ross groaned and turned his face to the wall. For this, he thought, he had come the better part of a hundred light years; for this he had left a comfortable job with a brilliant future. He spent a measurable period of time cursing the memory of old Haarland and his double-jointed, persuasive tongue.

Back in the days of Ross's early teens he had seen a good many situations like this in the tri-dis, and the hero had never failed to extricate himself by a simple exercise of superhuman strength, intellect, and ingenuity. That, Ross told himself, was just what he needed now. The trouble was, he didn't have them.

All he had was the secret of faster-than-light travel. And, here on Azor as on the planet of the graybeards, it had laid a king-sized egg. Women, Ross thought bitterly, women were basically inward-directed and self-seeking; trust them with the secret of F-T-L; make them, like the Cavallos, custodians of a universe-racking truth; and see the secret lost or embalmed in sterile custom. What, he silently demanded of himself, did the greatest of scientific discoveries mean to a biological baby-foundry? How could any female—no single member of which class had ever painted a great picture, written a great book, composed a great sonata, or discovered a great scientific truth—appreciate the ultimate importance of the F-T-L drive? It was like entrusting a first-folio Shakespeare to a broody hen; the shredded scraps would be made into a nest. For the egg came first. Motherhood was all.

That explained it, of course. That, Ross told himself moodily, explained everything except why the F-T-L secret had fallen into apparently equal or worse desuetude on such planets as Gemsel, Clyde, Cyrnus One, Ragansworld, Tau Ceti II, Capella's family of eight, and perhaps a hundred others.

Ragansworld was gone entirely, drowned in a planetary nebula.

The planet of the graybeard had gone to seed; nothing new, nothing not hallowed by tradition had a chance in its decrepit social order.

His home, Halsey's Planet, was rapidly, calmly, inevitably depopulating itself.

And Azor had fallen into a rigid, self-centered matriarchal order that only an act of God could break; but it wasn't any worse than any of the others.

So women were not the culprits.

The human race was.

Ross searched desperately in his mind for a pattern, for a clue to the meaning of the universal decay. If there was one, he couldn't find it. All he had gained for the sacrifice of his career was a few new question marks to add to the problem that had already loomed hopelessly huge back on Halsey's Planet. Perhaps there was no solution. Perhaps old Haarland had known that all along, had sent him out on a one-chance-in-a-million fool's errand.

None of that mattered, of course. What mattered was that he was in deeper trouble than ever, and with less hope of a way out for his own personal life. Still, it was better to keep analyzing and pondering than to listen to Bernie's endless whimpering complaints.

The trouble with that was that the image of Helena kept intruding itself between him and his thoughts.

He had dragged her into this mess along with him.

On the other hand, what did she have when he found her? What kind of a life was that?

But at least it was a life, he told himself, feeling a kind of guilt and a species of concern he had not thought himself capable of. Was he getting sentimental about that sweet little chucklehead? Who, he hastily added, had come near to criminally assaulting him. Who had left him alone for long, worried hours, while she was fooling around with Pilot Breuer and the easy-virtue lads at Virgin Willie's. Who—

Who was sweet and trusting and very, very feminine.

He turned to Bernie and demanded, "Will she be on the orbital station with us if we get convicted?"

"Who? Helena? Aw, no, they don't do that to women," Bernie explained. "*Minerva's* for males— and, oh, Ross, you don't know how rotten that's going to be—"

"Never mind that," snapped Ross. "I'm asking about Helena. What's the matter?" he added, struck by the man's suddenly opaque look.

"Well, it's just that she's foreign, see?" said Bernie. "If she was from around here they'd probably let her off pretty easy. It's only the real hard cases they do it to."

"Do *what* to?"

"The supreme penalty," Bernie said reluctantly.

He didn't really have to say more. His expression said it all.

"Oh, my God," said Ross. He swallowed. "How—how do they do it?" It was painful in ways he had never experienced before to think of Helena's slim young body jerking grotesquely at a rope's end, or jolting as she sat strapped in a huge, ugly chair.

Bernie had been watching him. "I'm sorry," the little man said soberly. "Of course, it's up to the judge. Maybe she'll go easy." But it was plain he didn't believe that. "Otherwise—otherwise—well, let's just hope they'll give Helena a quick-out pill, you know? That she can take whenever she wants to? Otherwise it's slow starvation out in space."

"Oh, my God," moaned Ross again. Slow starvation—

He looked up. "What do you mean, in space?"

"In her ship," Bernie explained. "What they'll do is put her back in it and fire it off with a keep-away. So the GCA won't bring her down again, you know? And she'll just stay out there forever." He stopped, puzzled. "What's the matter with you?" he demanded angrily. "Don't you like the kid? I'm telling you that she'd going to die out there!"

"Not necessarily," Ross snapped, searching his pockets frantically. "If only I can remember all the equations— If only there's a chance she can get that dim brain of hers to follow instructions—" He came up with a stylus and nothing else. "Have you got anything to write on?" he demanded.

"Yes, but——?" The waiter blankly passed over an order book. Ross sprawled on the floor and began to scribble: "Never mind how or why this works. Do it. You saw me work the big fan-shaped computer in the center room and you can do it too. Find the master star maps in the chart room.

Look up the co-ordinates of Halsey's System. Set these co-ordinates on the twenty-seven dials marked Proximate Mass. Take the readings on the windows above the dials and set them on the cursors of the computer——" He scribbled furiously, from time to time forcing himself deliberately to slow down as the writing became an unreadable scrawl. He filled the ruled fronts of the order pages and then the backs—perhaps ten thousand closely-written words, and not one of them wasted. Haarland's precise instructions, mercilessly drilled into him, flowed out again.

He flung the stylus down at last and read through the book again, ignoring the gaping Bernie. It was all there, as far as he could tell. Grant her a lot of luck and more brains than he privately credited her with, and she had a fighting chance of winding up within radar range of Halsey's Planet. GCA could take her down from there.

She knew absolutely nothing about F-T-L or the Wesley drive, but then—neither did he. That fact itself was no handicap.

He might rot on *Minerva*, but some word might get back to Haarland. And so would the ship. And Helena would not perish miserably in a drifting hulk.

Bernie saw the mysterious job was ended and dared to ask, "A letter?"

"No," Ross said jubilantly. "By God, if things break right they won't get her. It's like this——"

He happily began to explain that his F-T-L ship's rockets were only auxiliaries for fine maneuvering, but he counted on the court not knowing that. If he and Helena could persuade. . . .

As he went on the look on Bernie's face changed very slowly from hope to pity to politely-simulated interest. Correspondingly Ross's accounting became labored and faulty. The pauses became longer and at last he broke off, filled with self-contempt at his folly. He said bitterly, "You don't think it'll work."

"Oh, no!" Bernie protested with too much heartiness. "I could see she's awfully mechanically-minded for a woman, even if it wouldn't be polite to say so. Sure it'll work, Ross. Sure!"

The hell it would.

At least he had disposed of a few hours. And—perhaps some bungling setting would explode the ship, or end a Wesley Jump in the heart of a white dwarf star—sudden annihilation, whiffing Helena out of existence before her body could realize that it had died, before the beginning of apprehension could darken happy absorption with a task she thought would bring her to safety.

For that reason alone he had to carry the scheme through.

The courtroom was a chintzy place bright with spring flowers. Ross and Helena looked numbly at one another from opposite corners while the previous order of business was cleared from the docket. A wedding.

The judge, unexpectedly sweet-faced and slender though gray, obviously took such parts of her work seriously. "Marylyn and Kent," she was saying earnestly to the happy couple, "I suppose you know my reputation. I lecture people a bit before I tie the knot. Evidently it's not such a bad idea because my marriages turn out well. It's true that last week in Eleanor one of my girls was arrested and reprimanded for gross infidelity and a couple of years ago right here in Novj Grad one of my boys got five hundred lashes for nonsupport. Let's hope it did them some good, but those cases were unusual. My people, I like to think, know their rights and responsibilities when they walk out of my court, and I think the record bears me out.

"Marylyn, you have chosen to share part of your life with this man. You intend to bear his children. This should not be because your animal appetites have overcome you and you can't win his consent in any other way but because you know, down deep in your womanly heart, that you can make him happy. Never forget this. If you should thoughtlessly conceive by some other man, don't tell him. He would only brood. Be thrifty, Marylyn. I have seen more marriages broken up by finances than any other reason. If your husband earns a hundred Eleanors a week, spend only that and no more. If he makes *fifty* Eleanors a week spend only that and no more. Honorable poverty is preferable to debt. And, from a practical standpoint, if you spend more than your husband earns he will be jailed for debt sooner or later, with resulting loss to your own pocket.

"Kent, you have accepted the proposal of this woman. I see by your dossier that you got in just under the wire. In your income group the anti-bachelor laws would have caught up with you in one more week. I must say I don't like the look of it, but I'll give you the benefit of the doubt. I want to talk to you about the meaning of marriage. Not just the wage assignment, not just the insurance policy, not just the waiver of paternity and copulation 'rights', so-called. Those, as a good citizen, you will abide by automatically—Heaven help you if you don't. But there is more to marriage than that. The honor you have been done by this woman who sees you as desirable is not a sterile legalism. Marriage is like a rocket, I sometimes think. The brute, unreasoning strength of the main jets representing the husband's share and the delicate precise steering and stabilizing jets the wife's. We have all of us seen too many marriages crash to the ground like a rocket when these roles were reversed. It is not reasonable to expect the wife to provide the drive—that is, the income. It is not reasonable to expect the husband to provide the steering—that is, the direction of the personal and household expenditures. So much for the material side of things. On the spiritual side, I have little to say. The laws are most explicit; see that you obey them—and if you don't, you had better pray that you wind up in some court other than mine. I have no patience with the obsolete doctrine that there is such a legal entity as seduction by the female, despite the mouthings of certain so-called jurists who disgrace the bench of a certain nearby city.

"Having heard these things, Marylyn and Kent, step forward and join hands."

They did. The ceremony was short and simple; the couple then walked from the courtroom under the beaming smile of the judge.

A burly guard next to Ross pointed at the groom. "Look," she said sentimentally. "He's crying. Cute!"

"I don't blame the poor sucker," Ross flared, and then, being a man of conscience, wondered suddenly if that was why, in the old days at home, it had been women who cried at weddings.

A clerk called: "Dear, let's have those egalitarians front and center, please. Her honor's terribly rushed."

Helena was escorted forward from one side, while Ross and Bernie were jostled to the fore from the other. The judge turned from the happy couple. As she looked down at the three of them the smile that curved her lips turned into something quite different. Ross, quailing, suddenly realized that he had seen just that expression once before. It was when he was very, very young, when a friend of his mother's had come bustling into the kitchen where he was playing, just after she had smelled, and just before she had seen, the long-dead rat he had fetched up from the abandoned cellar across the street.

While the clerk was reading the orders, indictment and verdict, the judge's stare never wavered. And when the clerk had finished, the judge's silent stare remained, for a long, terrible time.

In the quietest of voices, the judge said, "So."

Ross caught a flicker of motion out of the corner of his eye. He turned just in time to see Bernie, knees buckling, slip white-faced and unconscious to the floor. The guards rushed forward, but the judge raised a peremptory hand, "Leave him alone," she ordered soberly. "It is kinder. Defendants, you are convicted of the gravest of crimes. Have you anything to say before sentence is passed on you?"

Ross tried to force words—any words, to protest, to plead, to vilify—through his clogged throat. All he managed was a croaking sound; and Helena, by his side, nudged him sharply to silence. He turned to her sharply, and realized that this was the best chance he'd be likely to get. He clutched at her, rolled up his eyes, slumped to the floor in as close an imitation of Bernie's swoon as he could manage.

The judge was visibly annoyed. This time she didn't stop the attendants when they rushed in to kick Ross erect. But he had the consolation of seeing a flash of understanding cross Helena's face, and her hand dart to a pocket with the paper he had handed her. In the confusion no one saw.

The rest of the courtroom scene was kaleidoscopic in Ross's recollection. The only part he remembered clearly was the judge's voice as she said to him and Bernie, "——for the rest of your lives, as long as Almighty God shall, in Her infinite wisdom, permit you the breath of life, be banished from Azor and all of its allied worlds to the prison hulk in Orbit Minerva."

And they were hustled out as the judge, even more wrathful than before, turned to pronounce sentence on Helena.

9

The prison-hulk guard teetered on the balls of her feet and spat disgustedly. "Fine lot of wrecks we're getting," she complained. "No action in them at all—'cept maybe the little one," she added, leering at Bernie, who quailed away. "Might as well be another damn batch of long-liners for all the work we'll get out of them, though. Not like the old days! They used to send real *men* here." She glowered at Ross and Bernie, nervously swallowing in the faintly nauseating pseudo-gravity of the satellite. She shook their commitment papers at them. "And for treason, too! Used to be it took guts to commit a crime against the state. Well, we'll knock that out of you easy enough." She shook her head again, then made a noise of distaste and scribbled initials on the commitment papers. She handed them back to the pilot who had brought them up from Azor, who grinned, waved, and got out of there. "All right," said the guard, "we have to take what we get. I'll have to put you two on construction; you'll never stand up under hard work. Keep your noses clean, that's all. Up at 0500; breakfast till 0510; work detail till 1950; dinner and recreation till 2005; then lights out. Miss a formation and you miss a meal. Miss two, and you get punishment detail. Nobody misses three.''

Ross and Bernie found themselves sharing a communal cell. They had all of five minutes to look around and get oriented; then they were out on their first work detail.

It wasn't so bad as it sounded. Their shiftmates were a couple of dozen ragged-looking wrecks, half-heartedly assembling a sort of meccano-toy wall out of sheets of perforated steel and clip-spring bolts. All the parts seemed well worn; some of the bolts hardly closed. It took Ross the better part of his first detail, whispering when the guards were looking the other way, to find out why. Their half of the prisoners were Construction; the other half was Demolition. What Construction in the morning put up, Demolition in the evening tore down. Neither side was anxious to set any speed records, and the guards without exception were too bored to care.

With any kind of luck, Ross found, he could hope eventually to get a real job—manning the *Minerva*'s radar, signal, or generating facilities, working in the kitchens or service shops, perhaps even as an orderly in the guard quarters. (Although Ross quite by accident chanced to see a guard's orderly as he passed through a corridor near the work area, a handkerchief held daintily to his nose. And though the orderly's clothing was neat and his plump cheeks indicated good eating, there was something about the expression in his eyes that made Ross think twice.)

The one thing he could not do, according to the testimony of every man he spoke to, was escape.

The fifth time Ross got that answer, the guard had stepped out of the room. Ross took the opportunity to thrash the thing through. "Why?" he demanded. "Back where I come from we've got lots of prisons. I never heard of one nobody escaped from."

The other prisoner laughed shortly. "Now you have," he said. "Go ahead, try. Every one of us has tried to figure out a way, one time or another. There's only one thing stopping you—there's no place to go. You can get past the guards easy enough—they're lazy, when they're not either drunk or boy-chasing. You can roam around *Minerva* all you like. You can even get to the spacelock, and if you want to you can walk right through it. But not in a spacesuit, because there aren't any on board. And not into the tender that brings us up from Azor, because you aren't built right."

Ross looked puzzled. "Not built right?"

"That's right. There's telescreens and remote-control locks built into that tender. The pilot brings you up, but once she couples with *Minerva* the controls lock. And the only way they get unlocked is when three women, in three different substations down on Azor, push the RC releases. And they don't do that until they look in their screens, and see that everybody who has turned up in the tender has stripped down to nothing at all, and every one of them is by-God female. Any further questions?" He grinned wryly. "Don't even think about plastic surgery, if that happens to cross your mind," he said. "We have two men here who tried it. You don't have much equipment here; you can't do a neat enough job."

Ross gulped. "Hadn't given it a thought," he assured the other man. "You can't even hide away in a trunk or something?"

The prisoner shook his head. "Aren't any trunks. Everything's one way—Azor to *Minerva*—except pilots and guards. No men ever go back. When you die, you go out the lock—without a ship. Same with everything else that they want to get rid of."

Ross thought hard. "What if they—well, what if you're sent up here and all, and then some new evidence turns up and you're found innocent? Don't they send you back then?"

"Found innocent?" The man looked at Ross pityingly. "Man, you *are* new. Hey," he called. "Hey, Chuck! This guy wants to know what happens if they find out back on Azor that he's innocent!"

Chuck exploded into laughter. Wiping his eyes, he walked over to Ross. "Thanks," he grinned. "Haven't had a laugh like that in fifteen years."

"I don't see that that's so funny," Ross said defensively. "After all, the judge can make a mistake, none of us is per—awk!"

"Shut up!" Chuck hissed, holding a hand over Ross's mouth. "Do you want to get us all in *real* trouble? Some of these guys would rat to the guards for an extra hunk of bread! The judges never make a mistake." And his lips formed the silent word: "Officially."

He let go of Ross and stood back, but didn't walk away. He scratched his head. "Say," he said, "you ask some stupid questions. Where are you from, anyhow?"

Ross said bitterly, "What's the use? You won't believe me."

Chuck nodded. "Maybe not," he said, starting to turn away. Ross laid a hand on his shoulder.

"But just for the record," he said, "I happen to be from a place called Halsey's Planet, which is a good long distance from here. About as far as light will travel in two hundred years, if that gives you an idea."

Chuck looked skeptical. "You're no long-liner," he growled.

"Me? Good God, no! No, I came in an F-T-L ship. Faster than light, that is. I told you you wouldn't believe me."

To Ross's surprise, Chuck didn't laugh again. He looked dubious, and he scratched his head some more, but he didn't laugh. To the other prisoner he said, "What do you think, Sam?"

Sam shrugged. "There was that stuff from the radar watch a while ago. Load of crap, I thought, but maybe it was this guy McIntyre was talking to. We'll never know, of course; the guards caught his transmission." He didn't have to say what had happened to McIntyre. His face said it. "Then there was Flarney. We could have been wrong there, Chuck."

Ross demanded, "Wrong about what?"

"Well," Chuck said hesitantly, "it's this old nut, Flarney. Dunno when he came here. Way before my time, and he was a big joke even then. He talked crazy, just like you. No offense," he added, "it's just that we all thought he'd gone space-happy. But maybe we're wrong. Unless——" his eyes narrowed "unless the two of you are both space-happy, or trying to kid us, or something."

Ross said urgently, "I swear, Chuck, there's no such thing. It's true. Who's this Flarney? Where does he say he came from?"

"Who can make sense out of what he said? All I
know is, he talked a lot about something faster
than light. That's crazy; that's like saying slower
than dark, or bigger than green, or something. But
I don't know, maybe it means something."

"Believe me, Chuck, it does! Where is this man—
can I see him?"

Chuck looked uncertain. "Well, sure. That is,
you can see him all right. But it isn't going to do
you a whole hell of a lot of good, because he's
dead. Died yesterday; they're going to pitch him
out into space sometime today."

Sam said conversationally, "This is when Whitker
flips, I bet. One week without his old pal Flarney
and he'll begin to look funny. Two weeks and he
starts acting funny. Three and he's talking funny
and the guards begin to crack down. I give him a
month to get shot down and heaved through the
locker."

Old pal? Ross demanded, "Who's this Whitker?
Where can I get in touch with him?"

"Him and Flarney were both latrine orderlies.
That's where they put the feeble old men, mop-
ping and polishing. Number Two head, any hour
of the day or night. Old buzzard has his racket—
we're supposed to get a hank of cellosponge per
man per day, but he's always 'fresh out'—unless
you slip him a saccharine ration every once in a
while."

Ross asked the way to Number Two head and
the routine. But it was an hour before he could
bring himself to ask the hulking guard for permission.

"Sure, sonny," she boomed. "I'll show you the
way. Need any help?"

"No, thanks, ma'am," he said hastily, and she

roared with laughter. So did the members of the construction gang; though the guard was laughing, she was watching them, too. He hurried on his way thinking dark and bloody thoughts.

"Whitker?" he asked a tottering ancient who nodded and drowsed amid the facilities of the head.

The old man looked up blearily and squeaked: "Fresh out. Fresh out. You should've saved some from yesterday."

"That's all right. I'm a new man here. I want to ask you about your friend Flarney——"

Whitker bowed his head and began to cry noiselessly.

"I'm sorry, Mr. Whitker. I heard. But there's something we can do about it—maybe. Flarney was a faster-than-light man. He must have told you that. So am I. Ross, from Halsey's Planet."

He hadn't the faintest idea as to whether any of this was getting through to the ancient.

"It seems Flarney and I were both on the same mission, finding out how and why planets were dropping out of communication. You and he used to talk a lot, they tell me. Did he ever tell you anything about that?"

Whitker looked up and squeaked dimly. "Oh, yes. All the time. I humored him. He was an old man, you know. And now he's dead." The tears leaked from his rheumy eyes and traced the sad furrows beside his nose.

"Yes?" Ross encouraged. "Can you tell me about it, Mr. Whitker?"

" 'Course I can tell you about it," the old man flared feebly. "You think I'm dumb or something? Fine feisty young man he was, Flarney. Full of ideas. Said he'd figured it out, whatever it was he was figuring out, and the only place he could get the answers was Earth, he called it. Never heard of the place, myself." He dragged a wad of cellosponge out of a crack between lockers and wiped his nose. "Oh, he was a great one," he cackled, the old eyes gleaming. "I was too, you bet! Raunchy young kid. Married to this big good-looking woman—well, when she started fooling around, what was I going to do?" he demanded fiercely. It was impossible to believe that this dodderer had ever done anything criminal enough to be sent to Minerva, in spite of what he said.

"Please, Mr. Whitker," Ross begged. "Try to remember exactly what he said."

The old man hiccuped and said promptly, "L-sub-T equals L-sub-zero e to the minus T-over-two-N." He beamed pridefully at remembering it.

That damned formula again! "But what does it mean, Mr. Whitker?" Ross coaxed. "Did he ever tell you?"

"You bet he told me! Only—" The old man looked surprised, then wistful. "Only I kind of don't remember now. Was it something about genes?" he asked himself hazily. "Generations? I don't remember. But you go to Earth, young man. Flarney said *they'd* know, and know what to do about it, too, which is more than he did. His very words, young man!"

Ross didn't dare stay longer. Furthermore he suspected that the old man's attention span had been exhausted. He started from the room with a muttered thanks, and was stopped at the door by Whitker's hand on his shoulder.

"You're a good boy," Whitker squeaked. "Here."

Ross found himself walking down the corridor with an enormous wad of cellosponge in his hand.

The bunks were hard, but that didn't matter.

Dormitories were the outermost layer of the hulk, pseudogravity varies inversely as the fourth power of the distance, and the field generator was conventionally located near *Minerva's* center. When your relative weight is one-quarter normal you can sleep deliciously on a gravel driveway. This was the dormitory's only attractive feature. Otherwise it was too many steel slabs, tiered and spotted too close, too many unwashed males, too much weary snoring. The only things in short supply were headroom and air.

Not everybody slept. Insomniacs turned and grunted; those who had given up the struggle talked from bunk to bunk in considerably low tones.

Bernie muttered from a third-tier bunk facing Ross's: "I wonder if she made it."

Ross knew what he meant. "Unlikeliest thing in the world," he said. "But I think she went fast and never knew what hit her." He thought of the formula and "They'd know on Earth—and know what to do about it, too." Earth the enigma, from which all planetary peoples were supposed to be derived. Earth—the dot on the traditional master charts, Earth—from which and to which no longliners ever seemed to travel. Haarland had told him no F-T-L ship had in recent centuries ever reported again after setting out for Earth. Another world sunk in barbarism? But Flarney had said—no; that was not data. That was the confused recollections of a very old man, possibly based on the confused recollections of another very old man. Perhaps it had got mixed up with the semilegendary origin story.

Poor sweet Helena! He hoped it had happened fast, that she had been thinking of some pleasant prospect on Halsey's Planet. In her naïve way she'd think it just around the corner, a mere matter of following instructions. . . .

So thought Ross, the pessimist.

In his gloom he had forgotten that a mere matter of following instructions was exactly what it was. In his snobbishness he never realized that he was guilty of the most frightful arrogance in assuming that what he could do, she could not. In his ignorance he was not aware that since navigation began, every new instrument, every technique, has drawn the shuddery warnings of savants that uneducated skippers, working by rote, could not be expected to master these latest fruits of science—or that uneducated skippers since navigation began have cheerfully adopted new instruments and techniques at the drop of a hat and that never once have the shuddery warnings been justified by the facts.

Up the aisle somebody was saying in a low, argumentative tone, "I saw the drum myself. Naturally it was marked Dulsheen Creme, but the guards here never did give a damn whether their noses were dull or bright enough to flag down a freighter and I don't think they've suddenly changed. It was booze, I tell you. Fifty liters of it."

"Gawd! The hangovers tomorrow."

"We'll all have to watch our steps. I hope they don't do anything worse than getting quietly drunk in their quarters. Those foot-kissing orderlies'll get a workout, but who cares what happens to an orderly?"

"They haven't been on a real tear since I've been here."

"Lucky you. Let's hope they don't bust loose tonight. It's a break in the monotony, sure—but those girls play rough. Five prisoners died last time."

"They beat them up?"

"One of them."

"What about the others? Oh! Oh, Gawd—fifty liters, you said?"

Bernie began to whimper: "Not again! Not those plug-uglies! I swear I'll throw myself through the spacelock if they make a pass at me. Ross, isn't there anything we can do?"

"Seems not, Bernie. Maybe they won't come in. Or if they do, maybe they'll pass you by. There certainly isn't any place to hide."

A raucous female voice roared through the annunciator: "Bed check five minutes, boys. Anybody got any li'l thing to do down the hall, better do it now. See you lay-terrr!" Hiccup and drunken giggle.

For the first time in his life Ross suddenly and spontaneously acted like a tri-di hero, with the exception that he felt like a silly ass through it all.

"Got an idea," he muttered. "Get out of your bunk." He pulled the wad of cellosponge, old Whitker's present, from his pocket and yanked it in half, one for him and one for Bernie.

The Pullover said faintly: "Thanks, but I don't have to——"

Ross didn't bother to answer. He was carefully fluffing the stuff out to its maximum dimensions. He unzipped his coveralls and began wadding them with cellosponge.

"I get it," Bernard said softly. He stepped out of his one piece garment and followed suit. In less than a minute they had creditable dummies lying on their bunks.

The others watched their activity with emotions

ranging between awe and envy. One giant of a man proclaimed grimly to whoever cared to listen: "These are a couple of smart guys. I wish them luck. And I want you guys to know that I will personally break the back of any sneaking rat who tips off a guard about this."

"Sure, Ox. Sure," came a muted chorus.

Arranged in a fetal sleeping position, face down, the dummies astonished even their creators. It would take a lucky look in a fair light to note that the heads were earless, fibrous globes.

"They'll do," Ross snapped. "Come on, Bernie."

They walked quietly from the dormitory in their singlet underwear toward the dormitory latrine—and past it. Into the corridor. Through a doorless opening into a storeroom piled with crates of rations. "This'll do," Ross said quietly. They ducked into a small cavern formed by sloppy issuing of stock and hunched down.

"The dummies will fool the bed check. It's only a sweep with a hundred-line TV system. If the guards do raid the dormitory tonight we'll have to count on them ignoring the dummies or thinking they're a joke or being too busy with other things to care. They'll be drunk, after all. Then in the morning things'll be plenty disorganized. We'll be able to sneak back into formation—and that'll be that for a matter of years. They can't often bribe the pilots with enough to guarantee a real ripsnorting drunk. Now try and get some sleep. There's nothing more we can do."

They actually did doze off for a couple of hours, and then were awakened by drunken war whoops.

"It's them!" Bernie wailed.

"Shut up. They're heading for the dormitory. We're safe."

"Safe!" Bernie echoed derisively. "Safe until when?"

Ross threatened him with the side of his hand and Bernie was quiet, though his lips were mumbling soundlessly. The guards lurched giggling past and Ross said:

"We'll sneak into the lockroom. There won't be anybody there tonight; at least we'll get a night's sleep."

"Big deal," grumbled Bernie, but he followed, complaining inarticulately to himself. Ross thought tiredly: All this work for a night's sleep! And saw, half-formed, the dreadful procession of days and nights and years ahead. . . .

They reached the lockroom and stumbled in breathlessly.

"Dearie!" Two guards, playing a card game on the floor with a ring of empty bottles around them, looked up in drunken delight. "Dearie!" repeated the bigger of the two. "Angela, *look* what *we've* got!"

Ross said stupidly, "But I thought all you guards would be off getting drunk somewhere."

The guard made a clumsy pass at fluffing up her hair and giggled. She waved to the flickering bright lights over the door. "Duty comes first, dearie, and we've got some damn docking to take care of. Angela, just lock that door, will you?" The other guard scrambled unevenly to her feet and weaved over to the door. It was locked before Ross or Bernie could move.

The big guard stood up too, leering at Bernie. "Wow!" she said. "New merchandise. Just be patient, dearie. We've got a little something to attend to in a couple of minutes, but we'll have *lots* of time after that."

Then things began to happen rapidly. There was Angela the guard, inarticulate, falling-down drunk; she waved bonelessly at a brightly flickering light on the far side of the lockroom. There was the other guard, reaching out for Bernie with one hand, pawing at a bottle with the other. There was Ross, a paralyzed spectator.

And there was Bernie.

Bernie's eyes bulged wide as the guard came toward him. He babbled hysterically, "No! Nonononono! I said I'd kill myself and I——"

He still-armed the big guard and leaped for the lock door. Ross suddenly came to life. "Bernie!" he bellowed. "Hold it! Don't jump!"

But it was too late. The one guard sprawling, the other staggering helplessly across the floor, Bernie was clear. He scrabbled at the lockwheels, spun them open. Ross tensed himself for the sudden, awful rush of expanding air; he leaped after Bernie just as Bernie flung the lock door open and jumped.

Ross jumped after.

There was no rush of air. They were not in space. Around them was no ripping, sucking void, no flaming backdrop of stars; around them were six walls and a Wesley board, and Helena peering at them wide-eyed and delighted.

"Well!" she said. *"That* was fast!"

Ross said, "But——"

Helena, hanging from the acceleration loops, smiled maternally. "Oh, it was nothing," she said. "Ross don't you think we're far enough away yet?"

Ross said hopelessly, "All right," and cut the drive. The starship hung in space in the limbo between stars. Azor, *Minerva*, and the rest were light-years behind, far out of range of challenge.

Helena wriggled free from the loops and rubbed her arms where the retaining straps had gripped them. "After all," she said demurely, "you *told* me how to run the ship, and *really*, Ross, I'm not quite *stupid.*"

Ross said, "But——"

"But what, Ross? It isn't as if I were some sort of brainless little thing that had never run a machine in her life. My goodness, Ross——" She wrinkled her nose. "*You* should remember. All those days in the dye vats? Don't you think I had to learn a little something about machines *there?*"

Ross swore incredulously. To compare those clumsy constructs of wheels and rollers with the subtle subelectronic flows of the Wesley force—and to make it work! He said, unbelievingly, "And the *Minerva* helped you vector in? They gave you the co-ordinates and radared your course?"

"Oh, Ross," Helena sighed patiently, "of course they *offered* to, but it wasn't really necessary. Don't you remember? You said it yourself, it was just a matter of giving the lock and dock command. Really, don't you think I can handle the *simplest* little thing by myself?" She turned to Bernie, who was staring dazedly around him. "Are you all right, dear?" she asked maternally.

Ross turned numbly away from the two of them. He faced the Wesley Christmas tree of controls. Don't question it, he told himself. Take a miracle for what it is. Maybe there is a God after all. God maybe wanted you out of the *Minerva*, and God moves in mysterious ways His wonders to perform.

Or Hers.

Anyway, they had to get going. There was no

problem about falling back to Azor with the keep-away in operation; if GCA bothered with them at all, it would be to maneuver them in the opposite direction. But they did have other problems. When the court exiled Helena in the starship they had methodically stripped the food locker entirely. And he was hungry already.

He put everything else out of his mind and began trying to calculate a setting.

Over his shoulder, Bernie said, "Going home, are you? Back to that place you call Halsey's Planet?"

Ross shook his head. "Not this time. There's nothing there, and anyway as long as I've got this far I'm going to try to finish the job." He frowned at the Christmas tree. "Only," he said, "there seems to be a problem."

"Problem, Ross?" asked Helena. "If you'd like me to help you—"

"Thank you, no," he said darkly. "Anyway, it's not the course. It's the place. According to that half-witted old moron—"

"Ross!" cried Helena, scandalized.

"—according to Flarney the place to go is Earth. Only I can't seem to find a setting." He puzzled over the board for a moment, trying to remember. "Maybe if I put it in search mode," he muttered, keying in the name and watching the lights dance and glow.

They kept on doing that for some time. "Well, maybe," offered Helena, "if we just went somewhere else long enough to replenish our supplies, dear, it would be better, because honestly I feel a little as though I'd like something to eat."

"Not necessary," said Ross triumphantly, as the board glowed green with a solution. "Wonder why it did that?" He shrugged and went back to calculating a setting. "Funny," he said, "but it seemed to have the same place listed a couple of different ways. Hell, anyway . . . here we go!"

10

It took Ross a while to learn a lesson, but once learned it stuck with him. He had learned one thing very surely. This time, he promised himself, *no spaceport*. No GCA. He would land the ship himself, rather than risk falling into unfriendly hands again.

There was, he told the others gravely, a certain element of danger in that, because he had never landed a spacecraft alone before. They glanced at each other nervously, but didn't object.

They sneaked into the solar system that held fabulous old Earth from far outside the ecliptic, where the chance of radar detection was least; they came to a relative dead halt a quarter million miles from the planet and cautiously scanned the surrounding volume of space with their own radar.

No ships seemed to be in space. Earth's solar system turned out to be a trivial affair, only five planets, scarcely a half-dozen moons among them.

None of the planets except Earth itself was anything like inhabitable.

"Hold tight," said Ross grimly, "I'm not so good at this fine navigation." He cautiously applied power along a single vector; the starship leaped and bucked. He corrected with another; and the distant sun swelled in their view plates with frightening rapidity. The alarm beeps bleated furiously, and the automatic cutoff restored all controls to neutral. All three of them had gone flying across the cabin, but no bones seemed to be broken.

Ross, sweating, picked himself up from the floor and staggered back to the panel. Helena said, "Ross, dear? If you'd like me to—"

"No," he said firmly, gazing at the board.

"Now, Ross," said Bernie, "let's think this over. I say Helena takes us down."

Ross shook his head disdainfully. "You don't understand. It's the captain's job. I'm the captain."

"Actually," Bernie said, "I think we ought to take a vote. See, by Azor standards Helena gets to make the decision. By her own planet I do, because I'm the oldest. By your own, according to what you tell me, it's majority rule. Anyway you look at it, Ross, Helena gets the job."

"These pettifogging legalisms," Ross began cuttingly—but stopped. There was something in the way the others were looking at him that told him they were not to be dissuaded. "Oh, well," he said bitterly, "we might as well be dead as the way we are. Go ahead, Helena. Just remember, I told you so."

He swallowed his pride and stood back. Helena took his place before the board, nibbling on one thumbnail while she stabbed, seemingly at random, at the course controls. She wasn't even calculating! He gripped the loops and closed his eyes, waiting for death.

It didn't come. He heard the shrill scream of thin air outside the ship as they penetrated the atmosphere, felt the violent shaking of deceleration. It went on for a long time. . . .

Then there was a punishing thump. His eyes flew open. Helena was looking at him apologetically. "You would have done it better," she lied, "but anyway we're down."

Ross lied, "Of course, but I'm glad you had the practice. Where—uh, where are we?"

Helena silently showed him the radar plot. Earth, it seemed, had a confusing multiplicity of continents; they were on one in the northern hemisphere, a large one as Earth's continents went, and smack in the middle of it. It was night on their side of Earth just then; and, by the plot, a largish city was only a dozen or so miles away.

"Okay," said Ross wearily, "landing party away. Helena, you stay here while Bernie and I——"

Helena said simply, "No."

Ross stared at her a minute, then shrugged. "All right. Then Bernie will stay while——"

"I will not!" said Bernie.

Clearly it was time for a showdown. Ross roared: "Who's the captain here, anyway?"

"You are," Helena said promptly. "As long as I don't have to stay here alone."

"Yeah," said Bernie.

Ross said, "Oh." He thought for a while and then said, "Well, let's all go." They thought it was a wonderful idea.

Earth wasn't a very unusual planet—lots of green sand and purple vegetation. Either the master star chart was wrong or the gravity meter was off; the chart, strangely enough, gave Earth's gravity as 1.000000 and the meter as 0.8952, a whopping ten per cent discrepancy. Further, the principal inert gas in Earth's atmosphere was, according to the master chart's planetary supplement, nitrogen; and according to the ship's instruments was thoroughly laced with neon. A terrific aurora polaris display constantly flickering in the northern sky bore that out.

But the gap between the chart and the facts didn't particularly worry Ross as they swung along overland. So the chart was off, or perhaps things had changed. This was—according to Flarney via Whitker—the place where people knew about the formula, where his questions would be answered. After this, he thought happily, it's off to Halsey's Planet and an unspecified glorious future, revered as the savior of humanity instead of a lousy Yards clerk pushing invoices around. And Helena, he thought sentimentally. . . .

He turned to smile at her and found she and Bernie were giggling.

"Listen, you two!" Captain Ross roared. "Haven't you learned anything yet? What's the good of us exploring if we stroll along with our silly heads in the clouds, not paying attention? Do you realize that this place may be as dangerous as Azor or worse?"

"Ross——" Helena said.

"Don't interrupt! What this outfit needs is some discipline—tightening up. You two have got to accept your responsibilities. Keep alert! Be on the lookout! Any single thing out of the ordinary may be a deathtrap. Watch for——"

Helena was looking not at Ross but over his

shoulder. Bernie was making strangled noises and pointing.

Ross turned. Behind him stood a mechanical monstrosity vaguely recognizable as a heavily-armed truck, its motor faintly humming. A man leaned darkly from the cab and transfixed them to the ground with a powerful spotlight. From the dazzling circle of light his voice came, hasty and furtive. "Thought it was two women and a man, but I guess you're the ones. Ugh, those faces on you! Yes, you're the ones. Get in. Fast."

The light blinked out. When their eyes adjusted to the dimmer illumination of the stars and the aurora display they saw a side door in the body of the truck standing open. Too, one of the long, slim gun barrels with which the truck seemed copiously supplied swiveled to cover them.

Ross stupidly read aloud a sign on the truck: "Jones Floor-Cover Company. Finest Tile on Jones. Wall-to-Wall a Specialty. 'Rugs Fit For a Jones'."

"Yeah," the man said. "Yeah, yeah. Just don't try to buy any. Get in, for Jones' sake! If I'd of known you were half-wits I wouldn't of taken this job for a million Joneses, cash. Get in!" His voice was hysterical and the gun covering them moved ominously. "If this is a frame——" he began to shrill.

"Get in," Ross said shakily to the others. They climbed in and the door slammed violently and automatically. Helena began to cry in a preoccupied sort of way and Bernie began a long, mumbling inventory of his own mental weaknesses for ever getting involved in this crackbrained, imbecilic, feeble-minded. . . .

There were windows in the truck body and Ross turned from one to another. He saw the guns on the cab telescope into stubs, the stubs fold into the mounts, the mounts smoothly descend flush with the sheet metal. He saw the cursing driver manipulate a dozen levers as the car began to glide across the green sand, purple-dotted with vegetation. Finally, through the rear window, he saw three figures racing across the sand waving their arms, rapidly being left behind. All he could make out was that they seemed to be two women and a man.

Helena was wailing softly, "——and I am *not* ugly and just because we're young and we're strangers isn't any reason to go around insulting people——"

From Bernie: "——fatheaded, goggly-eyed, no-browed, slobber-lipped, dim-witted——"

"Shut up," Ross said softly. "Before I bang both your heads together."

They stared.

"Thank you. We've got to think. What's this spot we're in? What can we do about it? I don't have any F-T-L contact name for Earth and obviously this fellow picked us up by mistake. I saw two women and a man—remember what he said?—just now trying to catch up with us. He seems to be some kind of criminal. Otherwise why a disguised gun-carrier? Why floor coverings 'but don't try to buy any'? And Jones seems to be the name of the local political subdivision, the name of the local deity and the currency. That's important. It points to a rigid one-man dictatorship—Jones, of course, or possibly his dynasty. What course of action should we take? Kick it around. Helena, what do you think?"

"He shouldn't have said we were ugly," she pouted. "Isn't *that* important?"

"Women!" Ross said grimly. "If you'll kindly

forget the trivial affront to your vanity perhaps we can figure something out."

Helena said stubbornly: "But he *shouldn't*. We're not. What if they just *think* we are because they all look alike and we don't look like them?"

Ross collapsed. After a long pause during which he tried and almost failed to control his temper he said slowly: "Thank you, Helena. You're wrong, of course, but it was a contribution. You see, you can't build up such a wild, far-fetched theory from the few facts available." His voice was beginning to choke with anger. "It isn't reasonable and it isn't really any help. In fact it's the God-damndest stupidest imitation of reasoning I have ever——"

"City," Bernard croaked, pointing. The jolting ride had become smoother, and gliding past the windows were green tiled buildings and street lights.

"Fine," Ross said bitterly. "We had a few clear minutes to think and now we find they were wasted by the crackpot dissertation of a female and my reasonable attempt to show her the elements of logical thinking." He put his head in his hands and tried to ignore them, tried to reason it out. But the truck made a couple of sharp turns and jolted to a stop.

The door opened and the voice of their driver said, again from behind a flashlight's dazzling circle: "Out. Walk ahead of me."

They did, into a fair-sized, well-lighted room with eight people in it whom they studied in amazement. Every one of the eight was exactly the same height—six feet. Every one had straight red hair of exactly the same shade, sprouting from an identical hairline. Everyone had precisely the same build—gangling but broad-shouldered. Their sixteen eyes were the identical blue under sixteen identical eyebrows. Head to toe, they were duplicates. One of them spoke—in exactly the same voice as the truckdriver's.

"So you want to be Joneses, do you?" he said.

"Absolutely impossible."

"But we took their money."

"Give it back. Reasonable changes, yes, but look at them!"

"We can't give it back. Look what we spent already. Anyway, Sam,——" It sounded like "Sam" to Ross. "——anyway, Sam, look at some of the work you've done already. You can do it. I doubt if anybody else could, but you can."

Ross felt his eyes crossing, and gave up the effort of trying to tell which Jones was speaking to which. Even the clothing was nearly identical— purple pantaloons, scarlet jacket, black cummerbund sash, black shoes. Then he noticed that Third-from-the-left Jones—the one who seemed to be named Sam—wore a frilly shirt of white under the scarlet jacket. Only a lacy edge showed at the open collar; but where his was white, the others were all muted pastels of pink and green.

Sam said coldly, "I know nobody else can do it. Anybody else! Who else *is* there?"

A Jones with a frill of chartreuse pursed his lips. "Well," he said thoughtfully, "there's Northside Tim Jones——"

"Northside Tim Jones," Sam mimicked. "Eight of his jobs are in the stockade right now! Paraffin, for Jones's sake—he still uses paraffin to mold a face!"

"I know, Sam, but after all, these people need help. If you won't do it for them, what's left?"

Sam shrugged morosely. "Well——" he said. Then

he shook his head, sighed, and came forward to look at the three travelers. With an expression of revulsion he said, "Strip."

Ross hesitated. "Hold it!" he said sharply to Helena, already half out of her coveralls. "Sir, there may have been some mistake. Would you mind explaining just what you propose to do?"

"The usual thing," Sam said irritably. "Fix your hair, build up your frames, level you off at standard Jones height. The works. Though I must say," he added bitterly, "I never saw such unpromising specimens in my life. How the Jones have you managed to stay out of trouble this long? Whose garrets have you been hiding in?"

Ross licked his lips. "You mean," he said, "you want to make us look more like you gentlemen, is that it?"

"*I* want!" Sam repeated in bafflement. Over his shoulder he roared, "Ben, what kind of creeps are you saddling me with?"

Ben, looking worried, said, "Holy Jones, Sam, I don't get it either. It was a perfectly normal deal. This guy came up to me in Jones's Joint and made a pitch. He knew the setup all right, and he had the money with him. Six hundred Joneses, cold cash; and it wasn't funny money, either." His face clouded. "I did think, though," he mentioned, "that he said two women and one man. But Paul Jones picked them up right at the rendezvous, so it must've been the right ones."

He glowered suspiciously at Ross and the others. "Come to think of it," he said, "maybe not. Tell you what, Sam, you just sit tight here for twenty minutes or so." And he hurried out of the room.

One of the other Joneses said curtly, "Sit down."

Ross, Bernie, and Helena found chairs lined up against a wall; they sat. A different Jones rummaged in a stack of papers on a table; he handed something to each of them. "Relax," he advised. Obediently the three spacefarers opened the magazines he gave them. When they were settled, most of the Joneses, after a whispered conference, went out. The one that was left said, "No talking. If we made a mistake, we're sorry. Meanwhile, you do what you're told."

Ross found that his magazine was called *By Jones*; it seemed to be a periodical devoted to entertaining news and gossip of sports, fashion, and culture. He stared at an article headed "Be Glad the People's Police Are Watching YOU!", but the words made little sense. He tried to think; but somehow he couldn't find a point at which to grasp the flickering mass of impressions that were circling through his brain. Nothing seemed to make a great deal of sense anymore; and Ross suddnly realized that he was very, very tired.

He closed his eyes. If this was fabled old Earth, it was just one more agonizing disappointment, no better than any of the others. A good deal worse, in fact—at least Halsey's Planet had had some kind of *tolerable* social structure! Decaying, sure. Worrisome, of course. But on Halsey's Planet a person had a chance for some kind of life without weird people taking him captive every five minutes. . . .

Not for the first time, he cursed the name of Haarland and all his kind.

It was half an hour and a bit more before the door flew open and half a dozen Joneses burst in. Three of them were strangers. Ross had no difficulty picking them out. For one thing, two of them were women. The third, though acceptably red-haired, tall and gangling, had a nose a full centimeter shorter than any of the others, and his hair was crisply curled.

"You're Peepeece!" snarled the first Jones. "Congratulations! You found what you were looking for. Now let's see you get out of here alive!"

"There's been some mistake," Ross began automatically, but stopped as Helena's heel crunched down on his instep.

"What are Peepeece?" she asked innocently.

"Good try!" applauded the Jones. "You want us to think you're crazy or feeble-minded, right? As though anybody on Jones wouldn't know what the People's Police are!"

"Of course that's true," nodded Helena agreeably, "but, you see, we don't come from Jones. We come from planets of a distant star—three different ones, as a matter of fact. I mean, you probably have figured that out already, because we surely don't look as nice as you do."

Silence for a moment. All the Joneses looked at each other. Then one of them said doubtfully, "It's a fact that they don't look like any Joneses I ever saw."

"I knew you'd see that," said Helena, dimpling. "Gosh! I wish we did! Anyway, this man here is Ross, and he has a faster-than-light spaceship. He comes from Halsey's Planet—"

Ross had to admit that Helena's act was getting across with the audience. Long before she had finished reporting their meeting, their flight to Azor, the escape from *Minerva*, and the flight here, most of the Joneses had put their guns away, and all were showing signs of stupefaction. "——And then," she finished, "we saw this truck, and that very good-looking man picked us up. And so we're here on Earth; and, honest to goodness, that's the exact truth."

There was silence while the Joneses looked at each other. Then the plastic-surgeon-type Jones, Sam with the white shirt front, stepped forward. "Hold still, my dear," he ordered. Helena bravely stood rigid while the surgeon raked searchingly through the roots of her hair, peered into her eyes, expertly traced the configuration of her ribs.

He stepped back, shaken. "One thing is for sure," he told the others, "they're not Peepeece. Not with those bones. They'd never get in."

Ben Jones beat his forehead and moaned. "How do I get into these things?" he demanded.

One of the female Joneses said shrilly, "We didn't expect anything like this. We're honest Jones-fearing Joneses and—"

"Shut up!" Ben Jones roared. "What about the other two, Sam? They all right too?"

"Oh, for Jones's sake, Ben," Sam said disgustedly, "just look at them, will you? Do you think the police would take in a five-inch height deviation like that one——" he pointed to Bernie——"or a half-bald scarecrow like that?" Ross, stung, opened his mouth to object; but swiftly closed it again. Nobody was paying much attention to him, anyhow, except as Exhibit A.

"So what do we do?" Ben demanded.

Sam shrugged. "The first thing we do," he said wearily, "is to take care of our, uh, clients here. We get them out of the way, and then we decide what to do next." He looked around at the other Joneses. "If you three will come this way," he said, "we'll finish up your job and get you back home. I needn't remind you, of course, that if you should happen to mention anything you've seen here to-night to the Peepeece it would——" His voice was cut off by the closing door before Ross could catch the nature of the threat.

Ben Jones stayed behind, scowling to himself. "You people got any Joneses?" he demanded abruptly.

"You mean money? Not any at all," Helena said honestly. Ross could have kicked her.

Ben Jones growled deep in his throat. "Always it happens to me!" he complained. "I suppose we're going to have to feed you, too."

"Well," Helena said diffidently, "we haven't eaten in a long time——"

Ben Jones swore to his god, whose name was Jones, but he stepped to the door and ordered food. While they were eating, Ben Jones sat watching them, refreshing himself from time to time with a greenish bubbling liquid out of a jug. He offered some to Ross; who clutched his throat as though he'd swallowed molten steel.

Ben Jones guffawed till his eyes ran. "First taste of Jones's Juice, hey? Kind of gets right down inside, doesn't it?" He wiped his eyes, then sobered. "I guess you people are all right," he admitted. "What I'm going to do with you I don't know. I can't take you to Earth, and I can't keep you here, and I can't throw you out on the street—the Peepeece would have you in the stockade in ten minutes."

Ross, startled, said, "Aren't we on Earth?"

"Naw," Ben Jones said disgustedly. "Didn't you hear me? You're on Jones, halfway between Jones's Forks and Jonesgrad. But you came pretty close, at that. Earth's about fifty miles out the Jones Pike past Jonesgrad, turn right at Jonesboro Minor."

Ross said bewilderedly, "The planet Earth is fifty miles along the Pike?"

"Not a planet," Ben Jones said. "It's an old city, kind of. Nobody lives there anymore; the Peepeece don't permit it. I've never been there, but they say it's kind of, you know, different. Some of the buildings——" he seemed actually to be blushing—— "are as much as fifteen, twenty stories high; and the walls aren't even all green. Excuse me," he added, looking at Helena.

Sam Jones returned and said to Ben, "It's all right. All finished. Trivial alterations. Maybe they could have gone along for the rest of their lives on wigs and pads—but we don't tell them that, do we? And anyway now they won't worry. Healy Jones, the older man, for instance. Very bright fellow, but it seems he was working as a snathe-handler's apprentice. Afraid to take the master's test, afraid to change his line of work—might be noticed and questioned." He heaved a tremendous sigh and poured himself a tremendous slug of the green fluid. Ben Jones gave Ross a cynical wink and shrug.

"Look at my hand!" the surgeon exploded. It was shaking. He gulped the Jones Juice and poured himself another. "Nothing physical," he said. "Neurosis. The subconscious coldly counting up my crimes and coldly imposing and executing sentence. I'm a surgeon, so my hand trembles." He drank. "Jones is not mocked," he said broodingly. "Jones is not mocked. Think those three are going to be happy? Think they're going to be folded in Jones's bosom just because they're Joneses externally now? No. Watch them five years, ten years. Maybe they'll sentence themselves to be hateful, vitriol-tempered lice and wonder why nobody loves them. Maybe they'll sentence themselves to penal servitude and wonder why everybody pushes them around, why they haven't the guts to hit back—Jones is not mocked," he told the jug of green liquid, ignoring the others, and drank again.

Ben Jones said softly to them, "Come on," and led them into an adjoining room furnished with sleeping pads. He said apologetically, "The doctor's nerves are shot tonight. Trouble is, he's too Jonesfearing. Me, I can take it or leave it alone." His laugh had a little too much bravado in it. "There's a little bit of nonJones in the best of us, I always say—but not to the doctor. And not when he's hitting the Jones juice." He shrugged cynically and said, "What the hell? L-sub-T equals L-sub-zero e to the minus T-over-two-N."

Ross had him by his shirt frill. "Say that again!"

Ben Jones shoved him away. "What's the matter with you, boy?"

"I'm sorry. Would you please repeat that formula? What you said?" he hastily amended when the word "formula" obviously failed to register.

Ben Jones repeated the formula wonderingly.

"What does it mean?" Ross demanded. "I've been chasing the damned thing across the Galaxy." He hastily filled Ben Jones in on its previous appearances.

"Well," Ben Jones said, "it means what it says, of course. I mean, it's obvious, isn't it?" He studied their faces and added uncertainly, "Isn't it?"

"What does it mean to you, Ben?" Ross asked softly.

"Why, what it means to anybody, pal. Right's right, wrong's wrong, Jones is in his Heaven, conform or else—it means morality, man. What else could it mean?"

Ross then proceeded to make an unmannerly nuisance of himself. He grilled their involuntary host mercilessly, shrugging aside all attempted diversions of the talk into what they were going to do with the three visitors. He ignored protestations that Ben was no Jonesologist, Jones knew, and drilled in. By the time Ben Jones exploded, stamped out, and locked them in for the night, he had elicited the following:

Everybody knew the formula; they were taught it at their mother's knee. It was recited antiphonally before and after Jones Meetings. Ben knew it was right, of course, and some day he was going to get right with Jones and live up to it, but not just yet, because if he didn't make money in the prosthesis racket somebody else would. The formula was everywhere: on the lintels of public buildings, hanging in classrooms, and on the bedroom walls of the most Jones-fearing old ladies where they could see its comforting message last thing at night and first thing in the morning.

From a book? Well yes, he guessed so; sure it was in the Book of Joneses, but who could say whether that was where it started. Most people thought it was just Handed Down. Way back during the war—what war? The War of the Joneses, of course! Anyway, in the war the last of the holdouts against the formula had been destroyed. No, he didn't know anything about the war. No, not his grandfather's time or his grandfather's grandfather's time. Long ago, that war was. Maybe there were records in the old museum in Earth. The city, of course, not some Jones-damned planet he never heard of!

After Ben Jones slammed out and the room darkened Helena and Bernie exchanged comforting words from adjoining sleeping pads, to Ross's intense displeasure. They fell asleep and at last he fell asleep still churning over the problem.

When he woke he found that evidently the doctor, Sam Jones, had stumbled in during the night and passed out on the pad next to him. The white frill was stiff and green with dried Jones Juice. Helena and Bernie still slept. He tried the door.

It was locked, but there was a tantalizing hum of voices beyond it. He put his ear to the cold steel. The fruits of his eavesdropping were scanty but alarming.

"——cut 'em down mumble found someplace mumble."

"——mumble never killed yet mumble prosthesis racket."

"——Jones's sake, it's their lives or mumble mumble time to get scared mumble Peepeece are you?"

And then apparently the speakers moved out of range. Ross was cold with sweat, and there was an abnormal hollow in the pit of his stomach that breakfast would never fill.

He spun around as a Jones voice croaked painfully: "Hear anything good, stranger?"

The surgeon, looking very dilapidated, was sitting up and regarding him through bloodshot eyes. "Your friends are talking about killing us," he said shortly.

"They are not really intelligent," Sam Jones said wearily. "They were just bright enough to entangle me to the point where I had to work for them—and to keep me copiously supplied with that green stuff I haven't the intelligence to use in moderation."

Ross said, "How'd you like to break away from this?"

Sam Jones mutely extended his hand. It trembled like a leaf. He said, "For his own inscrutable reason, Jones grants me steadiness of hand during an operation designed to frustrate his grand design. He then overwhelms me with a titanic thirst for oblivion to my shame."

"There's no design," Ross said in exasperation. "Or if there is, luckily this planet is a trifling part of it. I have never heard of such arrogant pipsqueakery in my life. You flyspecks in your shabby corner of the Galaxy think your own fouled-up mess is the pattern of universal life. You're wrong! I've seen life elsewhere and I know it isn't."

The doctor passed his trembling hand over his eyes. "Jones is not mocked," he croaked. "L-sub-T equals L-sub-zero e to the minus T-over-two-N. You can't fight *that*, stranger. You can't fight that."

Ross realized the man was crying silently behind his covering hand. "Oh, *hell*," he said in disgust. "I can't handle your primitive superstitions! Don't you understand? That's no revelation direct from God—from Jones, I mean. It's a scientific formula of some kind."

The doctor looked rebellious. "Watch your mouth," he said.

"Sorry, I can't spare the time. I've heard that same formula before. Twice. Once from a loonie out of a long-lines spaceship, once from somebody who knew even less about it than the loonie. It's not religion. It's *science*."

The doctor was looking at him with haunted eyes. He started to speak, then turned away, looking for the last drops of his bubbling green anodyne. "No!" Ross shouted. "Don't you understand anything at all?"

The doctor sank back on his sodden bedding. "I

understand you're trying to save your life," he sneered.

"I'll save yours, too, if you let me. What have you got now? Another six months before the DTs? Listen, doctor, how would you like to make a fresh start? Be free? Get free of your shaking hands and your guilt? Get away from these criminals—murderers!"

The doctor licked his lips. He said faintly, "If I dared—"

"You dare! Just get us out of here. Take us to the museum in Earth City—then we'll make a run for my ship and you'll be off this miserable planet forever."

"That's dangerous," the doctor protested. "Why not just head for the ship?"

"Because I won't go without finding out what I need to know! It's there somewhere—it has to be! Take me there. Get me records, facts, anything about the War of the Joneses. If there's any meaning at all to the formula it has to be related to that. There was a battle over its interpretation, right? We know who won. Let's find out what the other side said. Get me in there." He was thinking of the disgraceful war of fanaticism that had marred his own planet's history. The doctor's weak Jones jaw was firming up, though his eyes were still haunted. "Stall your killer friends, doctor," Ross urged. "Tell them you can use us for experiments that'll cut the cost of the operations. That ought to bring them around. And get me the facts!"

"To be free," the doctor said wistfully. He said after a pause, "I'll try. But——" And rapped a code series on the steel door.

11

The good part was that the gamble had worked! Ross, clutching at the door of the little car as it bounced over the rutty roads, could hardly believe it. But it had all gone as he had hoped: the doctor had taken the bait, had even bestirred himself long enough to double-talk the rest of the gang into letting them go off to Earth City—"to get some real good surgical procedures that are stored there." Amazingly, the gang had bought it . . . at least part way. For the bad part was that they had flatly refused to let Bernie and Helena come along.

"I wish they were with us," Ross complained.

The doctor said with weak belligerence, "Who do you think I am? Jones? I *had* to leave your friends behind. I had enough trouble getting those hoods to let me take *you* along. After all, I'm not a miracle worker."

Ross said sullenly, "Okay, okay." He glowered out of the car window and spat out a tendril of red hair that had come loose from the fringe surrounding his mouth. The trouble with a false beard was that it itched, worse than the real article, worse than any torment Ross had ever known. But at least Ross, externally and at extreme range, was enough of a Jones to pass a casual glance.

And what would Helena and Bernie be thinking now? He hadn't had a chance to whisper to them; they'd been just waking when the doctor dragged him out. Ross put that problem out of his mind; there were problems enough right on hand.

He cautiously felt his red wig to see if it was on straight. The doctor didn't seem to look away from his driving, but he said: "Leave it alone. That's the first thing the Peepeece look for, somebody who obviously isn't sure if his hair is still on or not. It won't come off."

"Umph," said Ross. The road was getting worse, it seemed; they had passed no houses for several miles now. They rounded a rutted turn, and ahead was a sign.

STOP!
RESTRICTED AREA AHEAD
WARNING: THIS ROAD IS MINED
NO TRAFFIC ALLOWED! DETOUR
"Trespassers beyond this point will be shot without further notice." Decree #404-5
People's Commissariat of
Culture and Solidarity.

The doctor spat contemptuously out the window and roared past. Ross said, "Hey!"

"Oh, relax," said the doctor. "That's just the Cultureniks. Nobody pays any attention to *them*."

Ross swallowed and sat as lightly as possible on the green leather cushion of the car. By the time they had gone a quarter of a mile, he began to feel a little reassured that the doctor knew what he was talking about. Then the doctor swerved sharply to miss a rusted hulk and almost skidded off the road. He swore and manhandled the wheel until they were back on the straightaway.

White lipped, Ross asked, "What was that?"

"Car," grunted the doctor. "Hit a mine. Silly fools!"

Ross squawked, "But you said——"

"Shut up," the doctor ordered tensely. "That was weeks ago; they haven't had a chance to lay new mines since then." Pause. "I hope."

The car roared on. Ross closed his eyes, limply abandoning himself to what was in store. But if it was bad to see what was going on, the roaring, swerving, jolting race was ten times worse with his eyes closed. He opened them again in time to see another sign flash past, gone before he could read it.

"What was that?" he demanded.

"What's the difference?" the doctor grunted. "Want to go back?"

"Well, no——" Ross thought for a moment. "Do we have to go this fast, though?"

"If we want to get there. Crossed a Peepeece radar screen ten miles back; they'll be chasing us by now."

"Oh, I see," Ross said weakly. "Look, Doc, tell me one thing—why do they make this place so hard to get to?"

"Tabu area," the doctor said shortly. "Not allowed."

"Why not allowed?"

"Because it's not allowed. Don't want people poking through the old records."

"Why not just put the old records in a safe place—or burn the damn things up?"

"Because they didn't, that's why. Shut up! Expect me to tell you why the Peepeece do anything? They don't know themselves. It isn't Jonesly to destroy, I guess."

Ross shut up. He leaned against the window, letting the air rush over his head. They were moving through forest, purplish squatty trees with long, rustling leaves. The sky overhead was crisp and cool looking; it was still early morning. Ross exhaled a long breath. Back on Halsey's Planet he would be getting up about now, rising out of a soft, warm bed, taking his leisurely time about breakfast, climbing into a comfortable car to make his way to the spaceport where he was safe, respected, and at home. . . . Damn Haarland!

At least, Ross thought, some sort of a pattern was beginning to shape up. The planets were going out of communication each for its own reason; but wasn't there a basic reason-for-the-reasons that was the same in each case? Wasn't there some overall design—some explanation that covered all the facts, pointed to a way out?

He sat up straight as they approached a string of little signs. He scanned them worriedly as they rolled past.

"Workers, Peasants, Joneses all——"
"By these presents know ye——"
"If you don't stop in spite of all——"
"THIS to hell will blow ye!"

"Duck!" the doctor yelled, crouching down in the seat and guiding the careening car with one hand. Ross, startled, followed his example, but not before he saw that "THIS" was an automatic, radar-actuated rapid-fire gun mounted a few yards past the last sign. There was a stuttering roar from the gun and a splatter of metal against the armored sides of the car. The doctor sat up again as soon as the burst had hit; evidently only one was to be feared. "Yah, yah," he jeered at the absent builders of the gun. "Lousy fifty-millimeters can't punch their way through a tin can!"

Ross, gasping, got up just in time to see the last sign in the series:

"By order of People's Democratic Council
Of Arts & Sciences, Small Arms Divison."

He said wildly, "They can't even write a poem properly. Did you notice the first and third line rhyme-words?"

Surprisingly, the doctor glanced at him and laughed with a note of respect. He took a hand off the wheel to pat Ross on the shoulder. "You'll make a Jones yet, my boy," he promised. "Don't worry about these things; I told you this place was restricted. This stuff isn't worth bothering about."

Ross found that he was able to smile. There was a point, he realized with astonishment, where courage came easily; it was the only thing left. He sat up straighter and breathed the air more deeply. Then it happened.

They rounded another curve; the doctor slammed on the brakes. Suspended overhead across the road was a single big sign:

THAT'S ALL, JONES!
——PEOPLE'S POLICE

The car bucked, slewed around, and skidded. The wheels locked, but not in time to keep it from sliding into the pit, road wide and four feet deep, that was dug in front of them.

Ross heard the axles crack and the tires blow; but the springing of the car survived. He was jarred clear in the air and tumbled to the floor in a heap; but no bones were broken.

Painfully he pushed the door open and crawled out. The doctor limped after and the two of them stood on the edge of the pit, looking at the ruin of their car.

"That one," said the doctor, "was worth bothering about." He motioned Ross to silence and cocked an ear. Was there a distant roaring sound, like another car following on the road they had traveled? Ross wasn't sure; but the doctor's expression convinced him. "Peepeece," he said briefly. "From here on we go on foot. The Peepeece won't follow beyond here, but if they see us they'll by-Jones *shoot* beyond here."

He led the way rapidly to a bend in the road, then slowed, looking around. "Yeah," he said, "this is the place. There's supposed to be some kind of museum up ahead. Maybe that's what you want."

"I hope so," muttered Ross, who was beginning to wonder just what he did want. Why had the Wesley board misled him? Earth wasn't supposed to be a city, it was supposed to be a planet. He allowed himself one quick, scary thought of Helena and Bernie, back with the bootleg plastic-surgery thugs. What had he got them into?

What had he got himself into, for that matter? They covered the last hundred yards to the crumbling old buildings at a trot and paused. "That's Earth?" Ross asked.

The doctor fanned himself and blew. "That's it," he said, looking around curiously. "Heard a lot about it, but I've never been here before," he explained. "Funny-looking, isn't it?" He nudged Ross, indicating a shattered concrete structure beside them on the road. "Notice that toll booth?" he whispered slyly. "Eight sides!"

Ross said wearily, "Yes, mighty funny! Look, Doc, why don't you sort of wander around by yourself for a while? That big thing up ahead is the museum you were talking about, isn't it?"

The doctor squinted. His eyes were unnaturally bright, and his breathing was fast, but he was making an attempt to seem casual in the presence of these manifold obscenities of design. He licked his lips. "*Round pillars*," he marveled. "Why, yes, I think that's the museum. You go on up there, like you say. I'll, uh, sort of see what there is to see. Jones, yes!" He staggered off, staring from ribald curbing to scatological wall in an orgy of prurience.

Ross sighed and walked through the deserted, weed-grown streets to the stone building that bore on its cracked lintel the one surviving word, "Earth." This was all wrong, he was almost certain; Earth *had* to be a planet, not a city. But still. . . .

The museum had to have the answers. If there were answers to be had.

On its moldering double doors was a large lead seal. He read: "Surplus Information Repository. Access denied to unauthorized personnel." But the seal had been forced by somebody; one of the doors swung free, creaking.

Ross invoked the forcer of the door. If *he* could do it. . . .

He went in and stumbled over a skeleton, presumably that of the last entrant. The skull had been crushed by a falling beam. There was some sort of mechanism involved—a trigger, a spring, a release hook. All had rusted badly, and the spring had lost its tension over the years. A century? Two? Five? Ross prayed that any similar mantraps had likewise rusted solid, and cautiously inched through the dismal hall of the place, ready for a backward leap at the first whisper of a concealed mechanism in action.

It was unnecessary. The place was—dead.

Exploring room after room, he realized slowly that he was stripping off history in successive layers. The first had been the booby-trapped road, lackadaisically planned to ensure that mere inquisitiveness would be discouraged. There had been no real denial of access, for there was almost no possibility that anybody would care to visit the place.

Next, the seal and the mantraps. An earlier period. Somebody had once said: "This episode is closed. This history is determined. We have all reached agreement. Only a dangerous or frivolous meddler would seek to rake over these dead ashes."

And then, prying into the museum, Ross found the era during which agreement had been reached, during which it still was necessary to insist and demonstrate and cajole.

The outer rooms and open shelves were testimonials to Jones. There were books of Jonesology—ingenious, persuasive books divided usually into three sections. Human Jonesology would be a painstaking effort to determine the exact physical and mental tolerances of a Jones. Anatomical atlases minutely gave femur lengths, cranial angles, eye color to an angstrom, hair thickness to a micron. Moral Jonesology treated of the dangers of deviating from these physical and more elastic mental specifications. (Here the formula appeared again, repeatedly invoked but never explained. Already it was a truism.) And Sacred Jonesology was a series of assertions concerning the nature of The Jones in whose image all other Joneses were created.

Subdivisions of the open shelves held works on Geographical Jonesology (the distribution across the planet of Joneses) and similar works.

Ross went looking for a lower layer of history and found it in a bale of crumbling pamphlets. "Comrades, We Must Now Proceed to Consolidate Our Victory"; "Ultra-Jonesism, An Infantile Political Disorder"; "On The Fallacy of 'Jonesism In One Country'." These Ross devoured. They added up to the tale of a savage political battle among the victors of a greater war. Clemency was advocated and condemned; extermination of the opposition was casually mentioned; the Cultural Faction and the Biological Faction had obviously been long locked in a death struggle. Across the face of each pamphlet stood a similar logotype: the formula. It was enigmatically mentioned in one pamphlet, which almost incomprehensibly advanced the claims of the Biological faction to supremacy among the Joneses United: "Let us never forget, comrades, that the initiation of the great struggle was not caused by our will or by the will of our sincere and valiant opponents, the Culturists. The inexorable law of nature, $L_T = L_o e^{-T/2N}$, was the begetter of that holocaust from which our planet has emerged purified——"

Was it now?

The entrance to a musty, airless wing had once been bricked up. The mortar was crumbling and a few bricks had fallen. Above the arched doorway a sign said Military Archives. On the floor was a fallen metal plaque whose inscription said simply *Dead Storage*. He kicked the loose bricks down and stepped through.

That was it.

The place was lightless, except for the daylight filtering through the violated archway. Ross hauled maps and orders and period newspapers and military histories and handbooks into the corridor in armfuls and spread them on the floor. It took only minutes for him to realize that he had his answer. He ran into the street and shouted for the doctor, hardly able to believe that he had found what he was looking for.

The surgeon materialized from the entrance of an ancient bus station, stepping carefully, his face bemused, like that of a man just coming out of the most explicit of pornographic films. "What? What?" he demanded. "Don't tell me the Peepeece are here!"

"No, nothing like that. It's good news, Doc! I think we've found it. The formula is about *genetics*!"

"Genetics?" the doctor repeated wonderingly. "But how can that explain anything?"

"Help me!" Ross begged. "Read! Go through this stuff with me—it's all here!" He tugged the doctor after him, past the crumbling bones of the last explorer, into that central chamber where the most ancient and secret of the documents lay. "Take that file over there," he ordered. "I'll start on this one. Read!"

Together they pored over the crumbling pages, occasionally reading choice bits aloud to each other. It was the surgeon who found the definitive text, a paper-backed booklet issued for the enlisted men of the Provisional North Continent Government Army. It was entitled *Why We Fight*.

"What is a Jones?" the pamphlet asked rhetorically. "A Jones is just a human being, the same as you and me. Forget the rumors you've heard. If someone tells you a Jones is supernatural or unkillable, laugh at him. They are not! The superstition arose because of the fact that one Jones looks almost exactly like every other Jones. Putting a bullet through one Jones in a skirmish and seeing another one rise up and come at you with a bayonet is a chilling experience; in the confusion of battle it may seem that the dead Jones rose and attacked. But this is not the case. Never let the rumor pass unchallenged, and never fail to report habitual rumor-mongers.

"How did the Joneses get that way? Many of you were too young when this long war began to be aware of the facts. Since then, wartime disruption of education and normal communications facilities has left you in the dark. This is the authoritative statement in simple language that explains why we fight.

"This planet was colonized, presumably from the quasi-legendary planet Earth. (The famous Earth Archives Building, incidentally, is supposed to derive its puzzling name from this fact.) It is presumed that the number of colonists was originally small, probably in the hundreds. Though the number of human beings on the planet increased enormously as the generations passed, genetically the population remained small. The same genes (heredity units) were combined and reshuffled in varying combinations, but no new ones were added. Now, it is a law of genetics that in small populations, variations tend to smooth out and every member of the population tends to become like every other member. So-called unfixed genes are lost as the generations pass; the end product of this process would theoretically be a population in which every member had exactly the same genes as every other member. This is a practical impossibility, but the Joneses whom we fight are a tragic demonstration of the fact that the process need not be pushed to its ultimate extreme to dislocate the life of a planet and cause endless misery to its dwellers.

"From our very earliest records there have been Joneses. It is theorized that this gangling red-headed type was well represented aboard the original colonizing ship, but some experts believe one Jones type and the workings of chance would be sufficient to produce the unhappy situation of type-dominance.

"Some twenty-five years ago Joneses were everywhere among us and not, as now, withdrawn to South Continent and organized into a ruthless aggressor nation. They made up about thirty per cent of the population and had become a closely knit organization devoted to mutual help. They held the balance of political power in every election from the municipal to the plantary level and virtually monopolized production and finance. There were fanatics and rabble-rousers among them who readily exploited a rising tide of discontent over a series of curbing laws, finally pushed through by a planetary majority, united at last in self-defense against the rapacity and ruthless self-interest of the Joneses.

"The Joneses withdrew en masse to South Continent. Some of those who remained behind sincerely wished the Joneses well; others scoffed at the secession as a sulky and childish gesture. Only a handful of citizens guessed the terrible truth, and were laughed at for their pains. Five years after their withdrawal the Joneses returned across the Vandemeer Peninsula with tanks, guns, and aircraft, and the war had begun.

"A final word. There has been much loose talk among the troops about the slogan of the Joneses, which goes $L_T = L_0 e^{-T/2N}$. Some uninformed people actually believe it is an invocation which gives the Joneses supernatural power and invulnerability. It is not. It is merely an ancient and well-known formula in genetics which quantitatively describes the loss of unfixed genes from a population. By mouthing this formula, the Joneses are simply expressing in a compact way their ruthless determination that all genes except theirs shall disappear from the planet and the Joneses alone survive. In the formula L_T means the number of genes after the lapse of T years, L_0 means the original number of genes, e means the base of the natural system of logarithms and N means number of generations."

The surgeon said slowly and with wonder: "So *that* was my God!" He stretched out his hands before him. The fingers were rock-steady.

Ross left him and paced the corridor uneasily. Fine. Now he knew. Lost genes in genetically small populations. On Halsey's Planet, some fertility gene, no doubt. On Azor, a male-sex-linked gene that provides men with the backbone required to come out ahead in the incessant war of the genders? Bernie was a gutless character. Here, all too many genes determining somatotype. On the planets that had dropped out of communication, who knew? Scientific-thought genes? Sex-drive-determining genes?

One thing was clear: any gene-loss was bad for the survival of a planetary colony. Evolution had——on Earth——worked out in a billion trial-and-error years a working mechanism, man. Man exhibited a vast range of variation, which was why he survived almost any conceivable catastrophe.

Reduce man to a single type and he is certain to succumb, sooner or later, to the inevitable disaster that his one type cannot cope with.

The problem, now stated clearly, was bigger than he had dreamed. And now he knew only the problem—not the solution.

Go to Earth.

Well, he had tried. There had been no flaw in his calculations, no failure in setting up the Wesley panel. Yet—this was Jones, not Earth; the city was only a city, not the planet that the star charts logged. And the planet, beyond all other considerations, was less like Earth than any conceivable chart error could account for. Gravitation, wrong; atmosphere, wrong; flora and fauna, wrong.

So. Eliminate the impossible, and what remains, however unlikely, is true. So there had been a flaw in his calculations. And the way to check that, once and for all, was to get back to the starship.

Ross wheeled and went back into the book room. "Doc," he called, "how do we get out of here?"

The answer was: on their bellies. They trudged through the forest for hours, skirting the road, hiding whenever a suspicious noise gave warning that someone might be in the vicinity. The Peepeece knew they were in the woods; there was no doubt of that. And as soon as they got past the tabu area, they had to crawl.

It was well past dark before Ross and the doctor, scratched and aching, got to the tiny hamlet of Jonesie-on-the-Pike. By the light from the one window in the village that gave any signs of life, the doctor took a single horrified look at Ross and shuddered. "You wait here," he ordered. "Hide under a bush or something—your beard rubbed off."

Ross watched the doctor rap on the door and be admitted. He couldn't hear the conversation that followed, but he saw the doctor's hand go to his pocket, then clasp the hand of the figure in the doorway. That was the language all the galaxy understood, Ross realized; he only hoped that the householder was an honest man—i. e., one who would stay bribed, instead of informing the Peepeece on them. It was beyond doubt that their descriptions had long since been broadcast; the road must have been lined with TV scanners on the way in.

The door opened again, and the doctor walked briskly out. He strode out into the street, walked half a dozen paces down the road, and waited for Ross to catch up with him. "Okay," the doctor whispered. "They'll pick us up in half an hour, down the road about a quarter of a mile. Let's go."

"What about the man you were talking to?" Ross asked. "Won't he turn us in?"

The doctor chuckled. "I gave him a drink of Jones Juice out of my private stock," he said. "No, he won't turn anybody in, at least not until he wakes up."

Ross nodded invisibly in the dark. He had a thought and suppressed it. But it wouldn't stay down. Cautiously he let it seep through his subconscious again, and looked it over from every angle.

No, there wasn't any doubt of it. Things were definitely looking up!

Ben Jones roared, "Just what the hell do you think you're doing, Doc?"

The doctor pushed Ross through the doorway

and turned to face the other Jones. He asked mildly, "What?"

"You heard me!" Ben Jones blustered. "I let you out with this one, and maybe I made a mistake at that. But I by-Jones don't intend to let you get out of here with all three of them. What are you trying to get away with anyhow?"

The doctor didn't change his mild expression. He took a short, unhurried step forward. *Smack.*

Ben Jones reeled back from the slap, his mouth open, hand to his face. "Hey!" he squawked.

The doctor said levelly, "I'm telling you this just one time, Ben. *Don't cross me.* You've got the guns, but I've got these." He held up his spread hands. "You can shoot me, I won't deny that. But you can't make me do your dirty work for you. From now on things go my way—with these three people, with my own life, with the bootleg plastic surgery we do to keep you in armored cars. Or else there won't *be* any plastic surgery."

Ben Jones swallowed, and Ross could see the man fighting himself. He said after a moment, "No reason to act sore, Doc. Haven't we always got along? The only thing is, maybe you don't realize how dangerous these three——"

"Shut up," said the doctor. "Right, boys?"

The other two Joneses in the room shuffled and looked uncomfortable. One of them said, "Don't get mad, Ben, but it kind of looks as if he's right. We and the doc had a little talk before you got here. It figures, you have to admit it. He does the work; we ought to let him have something to say about it."

The look that Ben Jones gave him was pure poison, but the man stood up to it, and in a minute Ben Jones looked away. "Sure," he said distantly. "You go right ahead, Doc. We'll talk this over again later on, when we've all had a chance to cool off."

The doctor nodded coldly and followed Ross out. Helena and Bernie, suitably Jonesified for the occasion, were already in the car; Ross and the doctor jumped in with them, and they drove away. Now that the strain was relaxed a bit the doctor was panting, but there was a grin on his lips. "Son-of-a-Jones," he said happily, "I've been waiting five years for this day!"

Ross asked, "Is it all right? They won't chase after us?"

"No, not Ben Jones. He has his own way of handling things. Now if we were stupid enough to go back there, after he had a chance to talk to the others without me around, that would be something different. But we aren't going back."

Ross's eyes widened. "Not even you, Doc?"

"Especially not me." The doctor concentrated on his driving. Presently he said, "If I take you to the rendezvous, can you find your ship from there?"

"Sure," said Ross confidently. "Do that, Doc. No detours. We want to be on our way."

"Ross—" said Helena.

"No arguments!" Ross cried. "Honestly, Helena, *try* to remember what's important! We have to get out of here, don't you understand that?"

"Oh, I do, Ross," she said, "only I'm kind of hungry again, you know? What I was thinking, don't you suppose there's some place we could get some food and take it on the ship? Because, really, they cleaned everything out back on Azor, if you remember, and I just can't face another one of those darned long trips without some little thing to eat. . . ."

"Oh," said Ross. "Ah. I see what you mean. Well, maybe you're right. Doc? If you could find a store of some kind on the way—"

Space had never looked better to any of them.

They hung half a million miles off Jones, and Bernie was cooking up a lunch for the four of them while Ross fumbled irritably with the Wesley board. He set up the integrals for Earth; the plot came out the same. He put the board in search mode and got the same coordinates for "Earth"— once again, the city, not the planet. This time he went further. He consulted the master star chart.

There it was. Earth. The planet, not the city. But the board had refused to accept it as a setting.

He threw his pencil across the cabin and swore. "I don't get it," he complained.

"It's probably broken, Ross," Helena told him seriously. "You know how machines are. They're always doing something funny just when you least expect it."

Ross bit down hard on his answer to that. Helena nodded. "It'll be all right," she said. "Come and eat, Ross! Then afterward, if you want me to, I'll fix it for you."

"You'll— You'll—" He rolled his eyes upward and allowed himself to be led to the table, where Bernie was spooning out helpings of what appeared to be some kind of stew.

"My, this is good," Helena said brightly. "Go ahead and taste it, Ross. And please stop worrying about this dumb old Earth. What does it matter if we can't get there?"

"Matter? It matters more than anything in the world! It's what this whole thing was all about!"

"Ah," she said wisely, "but I've been thinking, Ross, and I've got a suggestion. Why don't we just forget Earth? We can go back to Azor. Oh, I don't mean *forever*. Just for a few years, say, until we're old enough to go home—my home, you know—when we'll all be grownups and, oh, what fun we'll have there! And while we're on Azor I promise I'll take care of you. All of you."

Ross stared unbelievingly at her, then dropped his spoon. "Who can eat?" he moaned.

Helena pursed her lips. "You don't like my suggestion, do you?"

"No," he said carefully, "I don't like your suggestion. I want to go to *Earth*. I want to do it *now*. I want—" And then control snapped and he began to swear—at Helena, at Azor, at the starship, at Haarland and most of all at himself.

Helena turned her back pointedly. She said to Bernie and the doctor, "The way Ross acts sometimes you'd think he was the only one who'd ever run this thing. Why, my goodness, don't I know it acts funny now and then? Didn't I have exactly the same experience myself? If I fixed it once, I guess I can fix it again if I have to."

Ross stopped the flow of expletives in mid-stream. He looked at her as though she had suddenly appeared out of nowhere. "Helena?" he said. "What do you mean, you fixed it once?"

"Humph," she sniffed, still addressing the other two. "Now I suppose he thinks he can get around me, no matter how mean he's been."

Ross gritted his teeth. "Helena," he said in a strangled voice, "I apologize. Please tell me what you mean."

"Oh, all right," she said, forgivingly. "It wasn't anything, Ross. It's just that after I read all those dumb instructions you gave me and did everything you said, then I thought to myself, why should I run off and leave my friends in jail? So I tried the lock and dock command, only it wouldn't accept it—because I'd already set up the other, you see? So I poked around the inside of the machine and I found this thing marked *Reject Primary Objective*— and I fixed it!" she finished triumphantly.

"You fixed it," said Ross. He glanced from one to the other. "She fixed it," he repeated. "Helena? How did you fix it, exactly?"

"I just figured it out," she said with pride. "Here, I'll show you." She reached out for the board and, before Ross could stop her, had felt for two snaps, gave it a twist and lifted off the panel.

"Hey!" cried Ross in anguish. "Don't you know only a specialist-technician is allowed to even *touch* the inside of a Wesley board?"

"Oh, don't be silly, Ross. See? I just fixed it, right there!"

Ross, eyes glazed, robotlike, peered down where she was pointing. Down at the socket of the *Reject* switch, next to two delicately machined helices that were a basic part of the Wesley drive, wedged between an eccentric vernier screw and a curious crystalline lattice was—a hairpin.

He picked it out and stared at it for a long time. Then, slowly, he replaced the panel and put the board in search mode for Earth.

The coordinates for the planet flashed immediately before him.

Doggedly, without looking at any of the others, he began to set up his computations.

"Ross?" said Helena apprehensively, "you're not mad or anything, are you?"

Ross didn't answer. He didn't look up. He kept his attention firmly on what he was doing and didn't speak at all as he set the Wesley board up for the Earth jump.

Then he turned to Helena. She quailed before the look in his eye, but all he said was, "I'm really very tired. I think I'll lie down for a while. Wake me when we get there, one of you, won't you?"

12

Ross awoke, clearheaded and alert. Helena and Bernie were looking at him apprehensively.

He understood and said grudgingly, "Sorry I flipped. I didn't mean to scare you. Everything seemed to go black——"

They smothered him with relieved protestations that they understood perfectly and Helena wouldn't stick hairpins into the Wesley Drive ever again. Even if the ship hadn't blown up. Even if she had rescued the men from *Minerva*.

"Anyway," she said happily, "we're off Earth. At least, it's *supposed* to be Earth, according to the charts."

He unkinked himself and studied the planet through a vision screen at its highest magnification. The apparent distance was one mile; nothing was hidden from him.

"Golly," he said, impressed. "Science! Makes you realize what backward gropers we were."

Obviously they had it, down there on the pleas-

197

ant, cloud-flecked, green and blue planet. Science! White, towering cities whose spires were laced by flying bridges—and inexplicably decorated with something that looked like cooling fins. Huge superstreamlined vehicles lazily coursing the roads and skies. Long, linked-pontoon cities slowly heaving on the breasts of the oceans. Science!

Ross said reverently, "We're here. Flarney was right. Helena, Bernie, Doc—maybe this is the parent planet of us all and maybe it isn't. But the people who built those cities *must* know all the answers. Helena, will you please land us?"

"Sure, Ross. Shall I look for a spaceport?"

Ross frowned. "Of course. Do you think *these* people are savages? We'll go in openly and take our problem to them. Besides, imagine the radar setup they must have! We'd never sneak through even if we wanted to."

Helena casually fingered the controls; there was the sickening swoop characteristic of her ship-handling, several times repeated. As she jerked them wildly across the planet's orbit she explained over her shoulder, "I had the darnedest time finding a really big spaceport on that little radar thing— oops! —but there's a nice-looking one near that coastal city. Whee! That was close! There was one— sorry, Ross—on a big lake inland, but I didn't like——Now everybody be very quiet. This is the hard part and I have to concentrate."

Ross hung on.

Helena landed the ship with her usual timber-shivering crash. "Now," she said briskly, "we'd better allow a little time for it to cool down. This *is* nice, isn't it?"

Ross dragged himself, bruised, from the floor. He had to agree. It was nice. The landing field, rimmed by gracious, light buildings (with the cooling fins), was dotted with great, silvery ships. They didn't, Ross thought with a twinge of irritation, seem to be space vessels, though; leave it to Helena to get them down at some local airport! Still— the ships also, he noticed, were liberally studded with the fins. He peered at them with puzzlement and a rising sense of excitement. Certainly they had a function, and that function could only be some sort of energy receptor. Could it be—dared he imagine that it was the long-dreamed-of cosmic energy tap? What a bonus that would be to bring back with him! And what other marvels might this polished technology have to give them. . . .

Bernie distracted him. He said, "Hey, Ross. Here comes somebody."

But even Bernie's tone was awed. A magnificent vehicle was crawling toward them across the field. It was long, low, bullet-shaped—and with cooling fins. Multiple plates of silvery metal contrasted with a glossy black finish. All about its periphery was a lacy pattern of intricate crumples and crinkles of metal, as though its skirts had been crushed and rumpled. Ross sighed and marveled: What a production problem these people had solved, stamping those forms out between dies.

Then he saw the faces of the passengers.

He drew in his breath sharply. They were godlike. Two men whose brows were cliffs of alabaster, whose chins were strong with the firmness of steady, flamelike wisdom. Two women whose calm, lovely features made the heart within him melt and course.

The vehicle stopped ten yards from the open spacelock of the ship. From its tip gushed upward a ten-foot fountain of sparks that flashed the gamut of the rainbow. Simultaneously one of the godlike passengers touched the wheel, and there was a sweet, piercing, imperative summons like a hundred strings and brasses in unison.

Helena whispered, "They want us to come out. Ross—Ross—I can't face *them*!" She buried her face in her hands.

"Steady," he said gravely. "They're only human."

Ross gripped that belief tightly; he hardly dared permit himself to think, even for a second, that perhaps these people were no longer merely human. Hoarsely he said, "We need their help. Maybe we should send Doc Jones out first. He's the oldest of us, and he's the only one you could call a scientist; he can talk to them. Where is he?"

A raucous Jones voice bellowed through the domed control room: "Who wansh ol' Doc, hargh? Who wansh goo' ol' Doc?"

Good old Doc staggered into the room, obviously loaded to the gills by a very enjoyable backslide. He began to sing:

"In A.J. seven thirty-two
A Jones from Jones's Valley,
He wandered into Jones's Town
To hold a Jonesist Rally.
He shocked the gents and ladies both;
His talk was most disturbing;
He spoke of seven-sided doors
And purple-colored curbing——"

Jones's eyes focused on Helena. He flushed. " 'm deeply sorry," he mumbled. "Unf'rgivable vulgararrity. Mom'ntarily f'rgot ladies were present."

Again that sweet summons sounded from the waiting car.

"Pull yourself together, doctor," Ross begged.

"This is Earth. The people seem—very advanced. Don't disgrace us. Please!"

Jones's face went pale and perspiration broke out. " 'Scuse me," he mumbled, and staggered out again.

Ross closed the door on him and said, "We'll have to leave him. He'll be all right; nothing's going to happen here." He took a deep breath. "We'll all go out," he said.

Unconsciously Ross and Helena drew closer together and joined hands. They walked together down the unfolding ramp and approached the vehicle.

One of the coolly lovely women scrutinized them and turned to the man beside her. She remarked melodiously, "Yuhsehtheybebems!", and laughed a silvery tinkle.

Panic gripped Ross for a long moment. A thing he had never considered, but a thing which he should have realized would be inevitable. Of course! These folk—older and incomparably more advanced than the rest of the peoples in the universe—would have evolved out of the common language into a speech of their own, deliberately or naturally rebuilt to handle the speed, subtlety, and power of their thoughts.

But perhaps the older speech was merely disused and not lost.

He said formally, quaking: "People of Earth, we are strangers from another star. We throw ourselves on your mercy and ask for your generosity. Our problem is summed up in the genetic law L_T equals L_0 e to the minus T-over-two-N. Of course—"

One of the men was laughing. Ross broke off.

The man smiled: "Wha's that again?"

They understood! He repeated the formula, slowly, and would have explained further, but the man cut him off.

"Math," the man smiled. "We don' use that stuff no more. I got a lab assistant, maybe he uses it sometimes."

They were beyond mathematics! They had broken through into some mode of symbolic reasoning that must be as far beyond mathematics as math was beyond primitive languages!

"Sir," he said eagerly, "you must be a scientist. May I ask you to——"

"Get in," the man smiled. Gigantic doors unfolded from the vehicle. Thought-reading? Had the problem been snatched from his brain even before he stated it? Mutely he gestured at Helena and Bernie. Jones would be all right where he was for several hours if Ross was any judge of blackouts. And you don't quibble with demigods.

The man, the scientist, did something to a glittering control panel that was, literally, more complex than the Wesley board back on the starship. Noise filled the vehicle—noise that Ross identified as music after a moment. It was a starkly simple music whose skeleton was three thumps and a crash, three thumps and a crash. Then followed an antiphonal chant—a clear tenor demanding in a monotone: "Is this your car?" and a tremendous chorally-shouted: "NO!"

Too deep for him, Ross thought forlornly as the car swerved around and sped off. His eyes wandered over the control board and fixed on the largest of its dials, where a needle crawled around from a large forty to a large fifty and a red sixty, proportional to the velocity of the vehicle. Unable to concentrate because of the puzzling music, unable to converse, he wondered what the units of time and space were that gave readings of fifty and sixty for their very low rate of speed—hardly more than a brisk walk, when you noticed the slow passage of objects outside. But there seemed to be a whistle of wind that suggested high speed—perhaps an effect peculiar to the cooling-fin power system, however it worked. He tried to shout a question at the driver, but it didn't get through. The driver smiled, patted his arm and returned to his driving.

They nosed past a building—cooling fins—and Ross almost screamed when he saw what was on the other side: a curve of highway jammed solid with vehicles that were traveling at blinding speed. And the driver wasn't stopping.

Ross closed his eyes and jammed his feet against the floorboards waiting for the crash which, somehow, didn't come. When he opened his eyes they were in the traffic and the needle on the speedometer quivered at 275. He blew a great breath and thought admiringly: They had reflexes to match their superb intellects, of course. There *couldn't* have been a crash.

Just then, across the safety island in the opposing lane, there was a crash.

There was a blinding flash of blue light that drowned out details, but the very brief flash of vision Ross was allowed told him, incredibly, that a vehicle had attempted to enter the lane going the wrong way, with the consequences you'd expect. He watched, goggle-eyed, as the effects of the crash rippled down the line of oncoming traffic. The squeal of brakes and rending of metal was audible even above the thumping music: "Is this your car?" "NO!"

Thereafter, as they drove, the opposing lane was motionless, but not silent. The piercing blasts of strings and trumpets rose to the heavens from each vehicle, as did the brilliant pyrotechnic jets. A call for help, Ross theorized. The music was beginning to make his head ache. It had been going on for at least ten minutes. Suddenly, blessedly, it changed. There was a great fanfare of trombones in major thirds that seemed to go on forever, but didn't quite. At the end of forever, the same tenor chanted: "You got a Roadmeister?" and the chorus roared: "YES!"

Ross thought forlornly that the music must contain values and subtleties which his coarser senses and undeveloped esthetic background could not grasp. But he wished it would stop. It was making him miss all the scenery. After perhaps the fifteenth repetition of the Roadmeister motif, it ended; the driver, with a look of deep satisfaction, did something to the control board that turned off a subsequent voice before it could get out more than a syllable.

He turned to Ross and yelled above the suddenly-noticeable rush of air, "Talk-talk-talk," and gave a whimsical shrug.

During the moment his attention wandered from the road, his vehicle rammed the one ahead, decelerated sharply and was rammed by the one behind, accelerated and rammed the one ahead again and then fell back into place.

Ross suddenly realized that he knew what had caused those crumples and crinkles around the periphery of the car.

"Subtle," the driver yelled. "Indirection. Sneak it in."

"What?" Ross screamed.

"The commersh," the driver yelled.

It meant nothing to Ross, and he felt miserable because it meant nothing. He studied the roadside unhappily and almost beamed when he saw a sign coming up. Not advertising, of course, he thought. Perhaps some austere reminder of a whole man's duty to the race and himself, some noble phrase that summed up the wisdom of a great thinker. . . .

But the sign—and it had cooling fins—declared:
>   BE SMUG! SMOKE SMOGS!

And the next one urged:
>   BEAT YOUR SISTER
>   CHEAT YOUR BROTHER
>   BUT SEND SOME SMOGS
>   TO DEAR OLD MOTHER.

It said it on four signs which, apparently alerted by radar, zinged in succession along a roadside track even with the vehicle.

There were more. And worse. They were coming to a city.

Turmoil and magnificence! White pylons, natty belts of green, lacy bridges, the roaring traffic, nimble-skipping pedestrians waving at the cars and calling—greetings? It sounded like "Suvvabih! Suvvabih! Bassa-bassa!" The shops were packed and radiant, dazzling. Ross wondered fleetingly how one parked here, and then found out. A car pulled from the curb and a hundred cars converged on the spot, shrilling their sweet message and spouting their gay sparkles. Theirs too! There were a pair of jolting crashes as it shouldered two other vehicles aside and parked, two wheels over the curb and on the sidewalk.

"Suvvabih-bassa!" shouted drivers, and the man beside Ross gaily repeated the cry. The vehicle's doors opened and they climbed out into the quick tempo of the street.

It was loud with a melodious babble from speaker horns visible everywhere. The driver yelled cheerfully at Ross: "C'mon. Party." He followed, dazed and baffled, assailed by sudden doubts and contradictions.

It was a party, all right—twenty floors up a shimmering building in a large, handsome room whose principal decorative motif seemed to be cooling fins.

Perhaps twenty couples were assembled, who turned and applauded as they made their appearance.

The vehicle driver, standing grandly at the head of a short flight of stairs leading to the room, proclaimed: "I got these rocket flyers like on the piece of paper you guys read me. Right off the field. Twenny points. How about that?"

A tall, graying man with a noble profile hurried up and beamed: "Good show, Joe. I knew we could count on you to try for the high-point combo. You was always a real sport. You got the fish?"

"Sure we got the fish." Joe turned and said to one of the lovely ladies, "Elna, show him the fish."

She unwrapped a ten-pound swordfish and proudly held it up while Ross, Bernie, and Helena stared wildly.

The profile took the fish and poked it. "Real enough, Joe. You done great. Now if the rocket flyers here are okay you're okay. Then you got twenny points and the prize.

"Buster? You're a rocket flyer okay, ain't you?"

Ross realized he was being addressed. He croaked,

"Men of Earth, we come from a far-distant star in search of—"

"Nah, nah," said the profile crossly. "Jus' answer the question, okay?"

"We come from a far-distant star—"

"Hey," said one of the women. "Wait a minnit, okay? Hey, Buster, where you from again?"

"I come from Halsey's Planet, ma'am. My friends here are from planets of other stars, where—"

"Nah, stick to the point, okay. Myron? What about that? They don't come from around here!"

The man who had brought them said, visibly agitated, "Now you hold on a minnit, Debbie-Sue! It don't say nothin' about around here no place. What Myron read me, it just said go to the rocket field and bring back a rocket flyer, right?"

"Like a rocket flyer from the *field*, see? That's what it meant."

"It never said nothin' like that! Jeez, don'cha know how to play Treasure Hunt? You just got to do what it says, thassall!"

Myron said, "Don't let's get in no argument, okay? I got the job of being judge here, I get to say what's right. So whaddya say, Buster? You a rocket flyer or what?"

Ross looked wildly from one to another of the godlike ones. If he did not know from the evidence of their technology that they had to be superhuman he might have suspected they were no smarter than your average long-liner stumblebum. He said carefully, "The ship does have rockets, true. But its principle mode of propulsion is the nucleophoretic drive, as derived from the Wesley Effect."

"Gotcha!" cried Debbie-Sue.

Myron shushed her and frowned at Ross. "Stick to the point, like Debbie-Sue said. You sayin' you ain't no rocket flyer from around here, none of you?"

"No," Ross said. He furtively pinched himself. It hurt. Therefore he must be awake. Or crazy.

The profile was sorrowfully addressing a downcast Joe. "You should of asked them, Joe. You really should of. Now you don't even get the three points for the swordfish, because you went an' tried for the combo. It reely is a pity. Din't you ask them at all?"

Joe blustered, "He did say sump'm, but I figured a rocket flyer was a rocket flyer, and they come out of a rocket. Anyway, it *looked* like a rocket." His lower lip was trembling. Both of the ladies of his party were crying openly. "We tried," Joe said, and began to blubber. Ross moved away from him in horrified disgust.

The profile shook its head, turned and announced: "Owing to a unfortunate mistake, the search group of Dr. Joseph Mulcahy, Sc.D., Ph.D., got disqualified for the combination. They on'y got three points. So that's all the groups in an' who got the highest?"

"I got fifteen! I got fifteen!" screamed a gorgeous brunette in a transport of joy. "A manhole cover from the museum an' a las' month *Lipreaders Digest* an' a steering wheel from a police car! I got fifteen!"

The others clustered about her, chattering. Ross said to the profile mechanically: "Man of Earth, we come from a far-distant star in search of——"

"Sure, Buster," said the profile. "Sure. Too bad. But you should of told Joe. You don't have to go. You an' your friends have a drink. Mix. Have fun. I gotta go give the prize now." He hurried off.

A passing blonde, stacked, said to Ross: "Hellooo, baldy. Wanna see my operation?" He began to shake his head and felt Helena's fingers close like steel on his arm. The blonde sniffed and passed on.

"I'll operate her," Helena said, and then: "Ross, what's *wrong* with everybody? They act so young, even the old people!"

"Follow me," he said, and began to circulate through the party, trailing Bernie and a frankly terrified Helena, button-holing and confronting and demanding and cajoling. Nothing worked. He was greeted with amused tolerance and invited to have a drink and asked what he thought of the latest commersh with its tepid trumpets. Nobody gave a damn that he was from a far-distant star except Joe, who sullenly watched them wander and finally swaggered up to Ross.

"I figured something out," he said grimly. "You made me lose." He brought up a roundhouse right, and Ross saw the stars and heard the birdies.

Bernie and Helena brought him to on the street. He found he had been walking for some five minutes with a blanked-out mind. They told him he had been saying over and over again, "Men of Earth, I come from a far-distant star." It had got them ejected from the party.

Helena was crying with anger and frustration; she had also got a nasty scare when one of the vehicles had swerved up onto the sidewalk and almost crushed the three of them against the building wall.

"And," she wailed, "I'm hungry and we don't know where the ship is and I've got to sit down and—and go someplace."

"So do I," Bernie said weakly.

So did Ross. He said, "Let's just go into this

restaurant. I know we have no money—don't nag me please, Helena. We'll order, eat, not pay, and get arrested." He held up his hand at the protests. "I said, get arrested. The smartest thing we could do. Obviously somebody's running this place—and it's not the stoops we've seen. The quickest way I know of to get to whoever's in charge is to get in trouble. And once they see us we can explain everything."

It made sense to them. Unfortunately the first restaurant they tried was coin-operated—from the front door on. So were the second to seventh. Ross tried to talk Bernie into slugging a pedestrian so they could all be jugged for disturbing the peace, but failed.

Helena noted at last that the women's wear shops had live attendants who, presumably, would object to trouble. They marched into one of the gaudy places, each took a dress from a rack and methodically tore them to pieces.

A saleslady approached them dithering and asked tremulously: "What for did you do that? Din't you like the dresses?"

"Well yes, very much," Helena began apologetically. "But you see, the fact is——"

"Shuddup!" Ross told her. He said to the saleslady: "No. We hated them. We hate every dress here. We're going to tear up every dress in the place. Why don't you call the police?"

"Oh," she said vaguely. "All right," and vanished into the rear of the store. She returned after a minute and said, "He wants to know your names."

"Just say 'three desperate strangers,' " Ross told her.

"Oh. Thank you." She vanished again.

The police arrived in five minutes or so. An ex-

cited older man with many stripes on his arms
strode up to them as they stood among the shredded ruins of the dresses. "Where'd they go?" he
demanded. "Didja see what they looked like?"

"We're them. We three. We tore these dresses
up. You'd better take them along for evidence."

"Oh," the cop said. "Okay. Go on into the wagon.
And no funny business, hear me?"

They offered no funny business. In the wagon
Ross expounded on his theme that there must be
directing intelligences and that they must be at
the top. Helena was horribly depressed because
she had never been arrested before and Bernie was
almost jaunty. Something about him suggested that
he felt at home in a patrol wagon.

It stopped and the elderly stripe-wearer opened
the door for them. Ross looked on the busy street
for anything resembling a station house and found
none.

The cop said, "Okay, you people. Get going. An'
let's don't have no trouble or I'll run you in."

Ross yelled in outrage, "This is a frame-up! You
have no right to turn us loose. We demand to be
arrested and tried!"

"Wise guy," sneered the cop, climbed into the
wagon and drove off.

They stood forlornly as the crowd eddied and
swirled around them. "There was a plate of sandwiches at that party," Helena recalled wistfully.
"And a ladies' room." She began to cry. "If only
you hadn't acted so darn superior, Ross! I'll bet
they would have let us have all the sandwiches we
wanted."

Bernie said unexpectedly, "She's right. Watch
me."

He buttonholed a pedestrian and said, "Duh."

"Yeah?" asked the pedestrian with kindly interest.

Bernie concentrated and said, "Duh. I yam losted. I yam broke. I losted all my money. Gimme some money, mister, please?"

The pedestrian beamed and said, "That is real tough luck, buddy. If I give you some money will you send it to me when you get some more? Here is my name wrote on a card."

Bernie said, "Sure, mister. I will send the money to you."

"Then," said the pedestrian, "I will give you some money because you will send it back to me. Good luck, buddy."

Bernie, with quiet pride, showed them a piece of paper that bore the interesting legend Twenty Dollars.

"Let's eat," Ross said, awed.

A machine on a restaurant door changed the bill for a surprising heap of coins and they swaggered in, making beelines for the modest twin doors at the rear of the place. Close up the doors were not very modest, but after the initial shock Ross realized that there must be many on this planet who could not read at all. The washroom attendant, for instance, who collected the "dimes" and unlocked the booths. "Dime" seemed to be his total vocabulary.

By comparison the machines in the restaurant proper were intelligent. The three of them ate and ate and ate. Only after coffee did they spare a thought for Dr. Sam Jones, who should about then be awakening with a murderous hangover aboard the starship.

Thinking about him did not mean they could think of anything to do.

"He's in trouble," Bernie said. "*We're* in trouble. First things first."

"What trouble?" asked Helena brightly. "You got twenty dollars by asking for it and I suppose you can get plenty more. And I think we wouldn't have got thrown out of that party if—ah—*we* hadn't gone swaggering around talking as if we knew everything. Maybe these people here aren't very bright——"

Ross snorted.

Helena went on doggedly, "——not *very* bright, but they certainly can tell when somebody's brighter than they are. And naturally they don't like it. Would you like it? It's like a really old person talking to a really young person about nothing but age. But here when you're bright you make everybody feel bad every time you open your mouth."

"So," Ross said impatiently, "we can go on begging and drifting. But that's not what we're here for. The answer is supposed to be on Earth. Obviously none of the people we've seen could possibly know anything about genetics. Obviously they can't keep this machine civilization going without guidance. There must be people of normal intelligence around. In the government, is my guess."

"No," said Helena, but she wouldn't say why. She just thought not.

The inconclusive debate ended with them on the street again. Bernie, who seemed to enjoy it, begged a hundred dollars. Ross, who didn't, got eleven dollars in singles and a few threats of violence for acting like a wise guy. Helena got no money and three indecent proposals before Ross indignantly took her out of circulation.

They found a completely automatic hotel at nightfall. Ross tried to inspect Helena's room for comfort and safety, but was turned back at the threshold by a staggering jolt of electricity. "Mechanical house dick," he muttered, picking himself up from the floor. "Well," he said to her sourly, "it's safe. Good night."

And later in the gents' room, to Bernie: "You'd think the damn-fool machine could be adjusted so that a person with perfectly innocent intentions could visit a lady——"

"Sure," said Bernie soothingly, "sure. Say, Ross, frankly, is this Earth exactly what you expected it to be?"

Ross gave him a furious glare, but tempered it quickly: It was not, after all, Bernie's fault that they seemed to have landed themselves in a world of morons. "They can't all be like that," he said. "I'm nearly sure there's somebody around with all the answers—look at the technology!"

"Yeah," Bernie said patiently. "Do you suppose maybe there's a prison ship up there in orbit somewhere, like on Azor? Where they put the ones that really do the brainwork?"

Ross considered the possibility, then shook his head. He said wisely, "That's an outside chance, Bernie, and I'm glad you brought it up. But I doubt it. No, I think my plan is best. We go for the government. First chance we get. There's got to be a Congress somewhere around here, or maybe a Mayor or a Governor—some sort of authority. And I'm prepared to believe that they'll have the answers we want."

Bernie's expression was gloomy. "I hope you're right, Ross, only I know what government's like back on Azor, and I wouldn't say they were one whole lot smarter than anybody else."

"This isn't Azor," Ross said firmly, and that closed the subject.

The attendant moved creakily across the floor and said hopefully, "Dime?"

13

Their second day on the bum they accumulated a great deal of change and crowded into a telephone booth. The plan was to try to locate their starship and find out what, if anything, could be done for Sam Jones.

An automatic Central conferred with an automatic Information and decided that they wanted the Captain of the Port, Baltimore Rocket Field.

They got the Port Captain on the wire and Ross asked after the starship. The captain asked, "Who wan'sta know, huh?"

Ross realized he had overdone it and shoved Bernie at the phone. Bernie snorted and guggled and finally got out that he jus' wannit ta know. The captain warmed up immediately and said oh, sure, the funny-lookin' ship, it was still there all right.

"How about the fella that's in it?"

"You mean the funny-lookin' fella? He went someplace."

"He went someplace? What place?"

"Someplace. He went away, like. I din't see him go, mister. I got plenty to do without I should watch out for every dummy that comes along."

"T'anks," said Bernie hopelessly at Ross's signal.

They walked the street, deep in thought. Helena sobbed, "Let's leave him here, Ross. I don't like this place."

"No," said Ross.

Bernie growled, "What's the difference, Ross? He can get a snootful here as well as anywhere else."

"I said no!" Then, relenting, "It's not just Doc, don't you see? This is the place I've been looking for. If there are any answers—watch it!" They were in the middle of a street as one of the battleship-sized cars came rumbling by, chorus of horns blaring at them. They jumped for the sidewalk. As it reached the corner and turned into a stream of traffic there was a sudden shrieking of brakes. Ross winced, waiting for the sound of the crash; instead there was only a flash of blue light. Ross didn't even look up. He went on doggedly, "If there are any answers anywhere in the universe they're here. They have to be. All we have to do is find them."

Bernie stepped around two tussling men on the ground, ineffectually thumping each other over a chocolate-covered confection. "Yeah," he said shortly.

Helena was late for breakfast the next morning, but when she got there she was full of news. "You wanted government, Ross? Okay. You got government. It's in what they call Washington, and that's only forty miles from here. What you want is what they call a 'Senator'."

"I never heard of a Senator," Ross said suspiciously.

"You never heard of any of this, Ross," she pointed out. "And the way we get there is we drive. In a car. We get one right around the corner."

"How'd you find all this out?" he demanded.

"The desk clerk likes me," she said simply. "Now, pass me some of those things they call 'pancakes' and let's get moving."

"It won't work," said Ross.

But at the first test he was wrong, because the car salesman was only too happy to let them take the latest model of a Tornado Twelve right out of the showroom. "You sure you ain't no deadbeat?" he asked Bernie anxiously. " 'Cause I got orders not to let no deadbeats take no cars."

"Aw, no," said Bernie. "We ain't no deadbeats. We don't even *know* no deadbeats."

"That's all right, then," said the salesman in relief. "Now, don't you forget, you're gonna bring the money around tomorrow for sure."

"Course I am," said Bernie righteously, " 'cause I ain't no deadbeat." And the three of them walked away with the keys to the Tornado Twelve, while the manager and the salesman combined to open the great window onto the street.

Ross was wrong at the second test, too. "We'll never be able to drive that thing," he said darkly, shuddering at the sight of the dashboard with its two hundred dials, gauges and winking lights.

"Silly," smiled Helena gaily. "Don't you think that I can handle something like this? I mean, after an interstellar F-T-L ship?" And to Ross's surprise, she could. It turned out that there were only three things that mattered: You pushed this thing to go, this other thing to stop; and you turned that thing to turn. All the rest either made the seats move in any of half a dozen directions, worked the radio (commercials only, and all sounding pretty much the same) or made various lights go on and off, along with hot air, cold air, window openers and closers; or did even more arcane things that seemed to have no point at all.

For the first five miles Ross's heart was in his mouth, but somehow they survived Helena's un-skilled driving, even when she got onto the high-speed traffic on the south-bound highway. It wasn't all that high-speed, Ross discovered. The noise of wind blowing past the car was not real wind, but some sort of recorded sound, designed to make the passengers think they were going faster than they were. The great plume of fire that jetted from the front when Helena stepped on the brakes was not a rocket. It exerted no force at all; it was simply a pretty fireworks effect. There was really very little about the car that was very dangerous, for the all-around bumpers were superbly engineered. Even Helena did no more than dent the skirts in a few dozen places as she jockeyed for position—no more, at that, than any other of the myriad cars around them. Ross began to relax. Then, when Helena reported that the place they wanted to look for this "Senator" in was called "the Capitol," and when the signs led them directly to a great domed building with signs saying "the Capitol" all about it, Ross almost dared to begin to hope.

Once inside the building, it began well enough. "We'd like to see the Senator," Ross told a strik-ingly built brunette sitting at a desk marked "Information."

"Cer'nly," she said. "Name?"

"I'm Ross," he said. "This is Helena, and this—"

"No, no," the woman said. "You don't get what I'm sayin'. What I mean, *his* name. The Senator, you know? What Senator do you wanna see?"

As Ross opened his mouth to speak he was pressed out of the way by Bernie. "Duh," he said. "Like, what Senators have you got, you know?"

"Oh, we got lots," said the woman. "You gotta pick one. 'Course, they ain't all here now."

"Oh, I get ya," said Bernie. "We probably ought to see one that's here, like."

"That's a good idea," the woman applauded. "So, lessee. There's Senator Harry Hoagland, he's from Tennessee—"

"That's fine," said Bernie quickly.

"—on'y he's takin' his nap now. Or there's Senator Bobby St. Joe, 'cept he don't wanna see nobody today. He don't feel too good right now, account a he was over at the President's party las' night. No," she said thoughtfully, "I tell you, you better see Senator Sam Maeterlinck, from Florida. He likes to see people real good and he don't get too many chances because, you know, he's got that bad breath problem."

Ross was beginning to scowl again. "Excuse me," he began, then interrupted himself and whispered in Bernie's ear.

"Oh, yeah, I get ya," said Bernie, nodding. Then, to the receptionist, "See, like we got this problem. What we wanna do, we wanna talk to the smartest one there is, you know what I mean? We got this Treasure Hunt game goin' and that's what we got to do."

"Oh, sure," smiled the woman. "Why didden you say so? No, you got to see Senator Willy

Wicklow, from Kansas. He's a real brain, you bet. All the time readin' and all that—all kinds of stuff, comics and everything. He even read somethin' with no pictures in it once."

"Yeah," said Ross faintly. "Sounds real nice. Listen, though, I just remembered something. We'll get back to you," he said over his shoulder, as he began to lead the others away.

Wrong at the first two tests, but at the final test not wrong at all. On the way back to Baltimore Ross was too despondent even to say, "I told you so."

"Duh," said Bernie to the car salesman, "see, what happened, my wife didden like the car. She said I got to take it back."

"Aw," said the salesman sympathetically, "that's a real shame. She didden like it?"

"Nah. She said she wanted something, like, with more pezazz, you know? So I'm real sorry, but here's your keys back."

"That's okay," said the salesman wistfully, and even managed to wish them a nice day when he let them out the door.

It did not seem like a nice day. Ross walked along the street aimlessly, head down, trying to think of a way to solve the problem. He hardly heard when Bernie gasped.

Then Helena said: "Isn't that a silly way to put up a big sign like that?"

Ross looked up. "My God," he said. A gigantic metal sign with the legend, *Buy Smogs——You Can SMOKE Them*, was being hoisted across the street ahead. The street was nominally closed to traffic by cheerfully inattentive men with red flags; a mobile boom hoist was doing the work, and quite obviously doing it wrong. The angle of the boom arm with the vertical was far too great for stability; the block-long sign was tipping the too-light body of the hoisting engine on its treads. . . .

Ross made a flash calculation: When the sign fell, as fall it inevitably would, perhaps two hundred people who had wandered uncaringly past the warning flags would be under it.

There was a sudden aura of blue light around the engine body.

It tipped back to stability. The boom angle decreased, and the engine crawled forward to take up the horizontal difference.

The blue light went out.

Helena choked and coughed and babbled, "But Ross, it *couldn't* have because——"

Ross said: "It's them!"

"Who?"

Excitedly: "The people behind all this! The people who built the cities and put up the buildings and designed the machines. The people who have the answers! Come on, Bernie. I just seem to antagonize these people—I want you to ask the boom operator what happened."

The boom operator cheerfully explained that nah, it was just somep'n that happened. Nah, nobody did nothin' to make it happen. It was in case if anything went wrong, like. You know?

They retired and regrouped their forces.

"Foolproof machines," Ross said slowly. "And I mean really *fool* proof. Friends, I was wrong, I admit it; I thought that those buildings and cars were something super-special, and they turned out to be just silly gimcracks. But not this blue light thing. That boom *had* to fall."

Bernie shrugged rebelliously. "So what? So

they've got some kinds of machines you don't have on Halsey's Planet?''

"A different order of machines, Bernie! Believe me, that blue light was something as far from any safety device I ever heard of as the starships are from oxcarts. When we find the people who designed them——''

"Suppose they're all dead?''

Ross winced. He said determinedly, "We'll find them.'' They returned to their begging and were recognized one day by a gray-haired man who had been part of the ultimately winning team at the party. He didn't remember just who they were or where they were from or where he had met them, but he enthusiastically invited them to yet another party. He told them he was Hennery Matson, owner of an airline.

Ross asked about accidents and blue lights. Matson jovially said some o' his pilots talked about them things but he din't bother his head none. Ya get these planes from the field, see, an' they got all kinds of gadgets on them. Come on to the party!

They went, because Hennery promised them another guest—Sanford Eisner, who was a wealthy aircraft manufacturer. But he din't bother his head none either; them rockets was hard to make, you had to feed the patterns, like, into the master jigs just so, and, boy!, if you got 'em in backwards it was a *mess.* You got the blue lights and everything then! Where'd the blue lights come from? Well, they were like what happened when things went wrong, you know? Wheredja get the patterns? Look, mister, I'm gettin' kinda tired a this. We *always* had the patterns, an' don't spoil the party with all this talk-talk, will ya?

The party was not spoiled. It was a smasher. All

three of the visitors woke with headaches on Matson's deep living room rug.

"You did fine, Ross," Helena softly assured him. "Nobody would have guessed you were any smarter than anybody else here. There wasn't a bit of trouble."

Ross seemed to have a hiatus in his memory about most of the party.

The importance of the hiatus faded as time passed. There was a general move toward the automatic dispensing bar. It seemed to be regulated by a time clock; no matter what you dialed first thing in the morning, it ruthlessly poured a double rye with Worcestershire and tabasco and plopped a fair imitation of a raw egg into the concoction. It helped!

Along about noon something clicked in the bar's innards. Guests long since surfeited with the prairie oysters joyously dialed martinis and manhattans and the day's serious drinking began.

Ross fuzzily tried to trace the bar's supply. There were nickel pipes that led heaven knew where. Some vast depot of fermentation tanks and stills? Fed grain and cane by crawling harvest-monsters? Grain and cane planted from seed the harvest-monsters carefully culled from the crop for the plow-and-drag-and-drill-and-fertilize-and-cultivate monsters?

His head was beginning to ache again. A jovial martini-drinker who had something to do with a bank—a *bank!*—roared, "Hey, fellas! I got a idea what we can do! Less go on over to *my* place!"

So they all went, and that disposed of another day.

It blended into a dream of irresponsible childhood. When your clothes grew shabby you helped yourself to something that fit from your host of the moment's wardrobe. When you grew tired of one host you switched to another. They seldom remembered you from day to day, and they never asked questions.

Their sex was uninhibited and most of the women were more or less pregnant most of the time. They fought and sulked and made up and giggled and drank and ate and slept. All of the men had jobs, and all of them, once in a while, would remember and stagger over to a phone and make a call to an automatic receptionist to find out if everything was going all right with their jobs. It always was. They loved their children and tolerated anything from them, except shrewd inquisitiveness which drew a fast bust in the teeth from the most indulgent daddy or adoring mommy. They loved their friends and their guests, as long as they weren't wise guys, and tolerated anything from them—as long as they weren't wise guys.

Did it last a day, a week, a month?

Ross didn't know. The only things that were really bothering Ross were, first, nobody wouldn't tell him nothin' about the blue lights and, second, that Bernie, he was actin' like a wise guy.

There came a morning when it ended as it had begun: on somebody's living room rug with a headache pounding between his eyes. Helena was sobbing softly, and that wise guy Bernie, was tugging at him.

"Lea' me alone," ordered Captain Ross without opening his eyes. Wouldn't let a man get his rest. What did he have to bring them along for, anyway? Should have left them where he found them, not brought them to this place Earth where they could act like a couple of wise guys and keep getting in his way every time he came close to the blue-light people, the intelligent people, the people with the answers to——to——

He lay there, trying to remember what the question was.

"——*have* to get him out of here," said Helena's voice with a touch of hysteria.

"——go back and get that fellow Haarland," said Bernie's voice, equally tense. Ross contemplated the fragments of conversation he had caught, ignoring what the two were saying to him. Haarland, he thought fuzzily, *that* wise guy. . . .

Bernie had him on his feet. "Leggo," ordered Ross, but Bernie was tenacious. He stumbled along and found himself in the men's room of the apartment building. The tired-looking attendant appeared from nowhere and Bernie said something to him. The attendant rummaged in his chest and found something that Bernie put into a fizzy drink.

Ross sniffed at it suspiciously. "Wassit?" he asked.

"Please, Ross, drink it. It'll sober you up. We've got to get out of here—we're going nuts, Helena and me. This has been going on for weeks!"

"Nope. Gotta find a blue light," Ross said obstinately, swaying.

"But you aren't finding it, Ross. You aren't doing anything except get drunk and pass out and wake up and get drunk. Come on, drink the drink." Ross impatiently dashed it to the floor. Bernie sighed. "All right, Ross," he said wearily. "Helena can run the ship; we're taking off."

"Go 'head."

"Good-by, Ross. We're going back to Halsey's Planet, where you came from. Maybe Haarland can tell us what to do."

"Go 'head. *That* wise guy!" Ross sneered.

The attendant was watching dubiously as Bernie slammed out and Ross peered at himself in a mirror. "Dime?" the attendant asked in his tired voice. Ross gave him one and went back to the party.

Somehow it was not much fun.

He shuffled back to the bar. The boilermaker didn't taste too good. He set it down and glowered around the room. The party was back in swing already; Helena and Bernie were nowhere in sight. Let them go, then. . . .

He drank, but only when he reminded himself to. This party had become a costume ball; one of the men lurched out of the room and staggered back guffawing. "Looka him!" one of the women shrieked. "He got a woman's hat on! Horace, you get the craziest kinda ideas!"

Ross glowered. He suddenly realized that, while he wasn't exactly sober, he wasn't drunk either. Those soreheads, they had to go and spoil the party. . . .

He began abruptly to get less drunk yet. Back to Halsey's Planet, they said? Ask Haarland what to do, they said? Leave him here——?

He was cold sober.

He found a telephone. The automatic Central checked the automatic Information and got him the Captain of the Port, Baltimore Rocket Field. The Captain was helpful and sympathetic; caught by the tense note in Ross's voice when he told him who wannit to know, the Captain said, "Gee, buddy, if I'd a known I woulda stopped them. Stoled your ship, is that what they done? They could get arrested for that. You could call the cops an' maybe they could do something——"

Ross didn't bother to explain. He hung up.

The party was no longer any fun at all. He left it.

Ross walked along the street, hating himself. He couldn't hate Helena and Bernie; they had done the right thing. It had been his fault, all the way down the line. He'd been acting like a silly child; he'd had a job of work to do, and he let himself be sidetracked by a crazy round of drinking and parties.

Of course, he told himself, something had been accomplished. Somebody had built the machines—not the happy morons he had been playing with. Somebody had invented whatever it was that flared with blue light and repaired the idiot errors the morons made. Somebody, somewhere.

Where?

Well, he had some information. All negative. At the parties had been soldiers and politicians and industrialists and clergy and entertainers and, heaven save the mark, scientists. And none of them had had the wit to do more than push the Number Three Button when the Green Light A blinked, by rote. None of them could have given him the answer to the question that threatened to end human domination over the cosmos; none of them would have known what the words meant.

Maybe—Ross made himself face it—maybe there was no answer. Maybe even if he found the intellects that lurked beneath the surface on this ancient planet, they could not or would not tell him what he wanted to know. Maybe the intellects didn't exist.

Maybe he was all wrong in all of his assumptions; maybe he was wasting his time. But, he told himself wryly, he had fixed it for himself that time was all he had left. He might as well waste it. He might as well go right on looking. . . .

A migrant party was staggering down the street toward him, a score of persons going from one host's home to another. He crossed to avoid them. They were singing drunkenly.

Ross looked at them with the distaste of the recently reformed. One of the voices raised in song caught his ear:

"——bobbed his nose and dyed it rose,
And kissed his lady fair,
And set her down on a cushion brown
In a seven-legged chair.
'By Jones,' he said, 'my shoes are red,
And so's my overcoat,
And with buttons nine in a zigzag line,
I'll——"

"Doc!" Ross bellowed. "Doc Jones! For God's sake, come over here!"

They got rid of the rest of Doctor Sam Jones's party, and Ross sobered the doctor up in an all-night restaurant. It wasn't hard; the doctor had had plenty of practice.

Ross filled him in, carefully explaining why Bernie and Helena had left him. Doc Jones filled Ross in. He didn't have much to tell. He had come to in the ship, waited around until he got hungry, fallen into a conversation with a rocket pilot on the field—and that was how *his* round of parties had begun.

Like Ross, Doc, in his soberer moments, had come to the conclusion that Earth was run by person or persons unseen. He had learned little that Ross hadn't found out or deduced. The blue lights had bothered him, too; he'd asked the pilot about it, and found out about what Ross had—there appeared to be some sort of built-in safety device which kept the inevitable accidents from becoming unduly fatal. How they worked, he didn't know—

He did not, in fact, know any more than Ross did. Which was nothing.

Ross sighed. "So we pulled a big, fat zero," he said.

"I guess so, Ross. Only—" His voice died away.

Ross waited politely, then said morosely, "I don't think I even believe there's any answer at all any more. Maybe the whole process has just gone too far. Maybe it's irreversible, whatever it is. Maybe all the good genes have decayed and disappeared."

"That's possible, medically speaking," the doctor agreed, "only—"

Ross waited again, then eyed the doctor suspiciously. "Come on, Doc. What is it you're holding back?"

The doctor looked embarrassed. "You'll think it's stupid," he said.

"Damned if I will! Doc, I'm *desperate*. Try me!"

"Well— There's a video program I heard about."

Ross was startled and showed it. "A *video* program? What kind of video program?"

The doctor shrugged. "I know it sounds ridiculous. One of the fellows was telling me about it. You go on the program and they guarantee to solve your problem. *Any* problem. You just go there, and they'll solve it."

Ross strained to control his irritation. "Doc," he began, "that is the dumbest thing I ever—"

The doctor sat mute.

"I mean, *really*, Doc—"

The doctor shrugged, flushing.

"Do you really think anything these dummies say is going to be worth *anything*?" Ross demanded, and at last the doctor began to change over from embarrassed to irritated.

"I *told* you you'd say that, Ross. I think it myself. Only—have you got any better ideas?"

"Well, no, but—" Ross stopped, thinking it over. "It's dumb," he said.

"Right, Ross."

"But, as you say, I don't have any better ideas. Tell me about this program."

"There's not much to tell. It's what I said. They guarantee to solve your problem, whatever. There's even some sort of bond posted. I don't know much about the details. The guy I was talking to said that was just a formality. They never failed. Of course," Doc finished, hearing his own proposal with a touch of doubt, "I don't know whether they ever had any problem like this before, but——"

"Yeah," said Ross. "What have we got to lose?"

They got into the program. It took the techniques of a doubler on an army chow line and a fair amount of brute strength, but they got to the head of the queue at the studio and wedged themselves inside. Doc came close to throttling the man who prowled through the studio audience, selecting the lucky few who would get on stage—but they got on.

The theme music swelled majestically around them, and a chorus crooned, "What's Biting You— Hunh?" It was repeated three times, with crashing cymbals under the "Hunh?"

Ross listened to the beginning of the program and cursed himself for being persuaded into such a harebrained tactic. But, he had to admit, the program offered the only possibility in sight. The central figure was a huge, jovially grinning figure of papier-mâché, smoking a Smog and billowing smoke rings at the audience. An announcer, for some obscure reason in blackface, interviewed the disturbed derelicts who came before Smiley Smog, the papier-mâché figure, and propounded their problems to Smiley in a sort of doggerel. And in doggerel the answers came back.

The first person to go up before Smiley was a woman, clearly in her last month of pregnancy. The announcer introduced her to the audience and begged for a real loud holler of hello for this poor mizzuble li'l girl. "Awright, honey," he said. "You just step right up here an' let ol' Uncle Smiley take care a your troubles for you. Less go, now. What's Bitin' You?"

"Uh," she sobbed, "it's like I'm gonna have a baby."

"Hoddya like that!" the announcer screamed. "She's gonna have a *baby!* Whaddya say to that, folks?" The audience shrieked hysterically. "Awright, honey," the announcer said. "So you're gonna have a baby, so what's bitin' you about that?"

"It's my husband," the woman sniffled. "He don't like kids. We got eight already," she explained. "Jack, he says if we have one more kid he's gonna take off an' marry somebody else."

"He's gonna marry somebody else!" the announcer howled. "Hoddya like that, folks?" There was a tempest of boos. "Awright, now," the announcer said, "you just sit there, honey, while I tell ol' Uncle Smiley about this. Ya ready? Listen:

What's bitin' this lady is plain to see:

Her husband don't want no more family!"

The huge figure's head rotated on a concealed hinge to look down on the woman. From a squawk-box deep in Smiley's papier-mâché belly, a weary voice declaimed:

"If one more baby is your husband's dread,
Cross him up, lady. Have twins instead!"

The audience roared its approval. The announcer asked anxiously, "Ya get it? When ya get into the hospital, like, ya jus' tell the nurse ya want to take *two* kids home with you. See?"

The grateful woman staggered away. Ross gave Doc a poisonous look.

"What else is there to do?" the doctor hissed. "All right, perhaps this won't work out—but let's try!" He half rose, and staggered against the man next to him, who was already starting toward the announcer. "Go on, Ross," Doc hissed venomously, blocking off the other man.

Ross went. What else was there to do?

"What's biting me," he said belligerently before the announcer could put him through the preliminaries, "is simply this: L-sub-T equals L-sub-zero e to the minus-T-over-two-N."

Dead silence in the studio. The announcer quavered, "Wh-what was that again, buddy?"

"I said," Ross repeated firmly, "L-sub-T equals L-sub-zero e to the——"

"Now, wait a minute, buddy," the announcer ordered. "We never had no stuff like that on *this* program before. Whaddya, some kind of a wise guy?"

There might have been violence; the conditions were right for it. But Uncle Smiley Smog saved the day.

The papier-mâché figure puffed a blinding series of smoke rings at Ross. From its molded torso, the weary voice said:

"If you're looking for counsel sagacious and wise,
The price is ten cents. It's right under your eyes."

They left the studio in a storm of animosity.

"Maybe we could have collected the forfeit," Doc said hopefully.

"Maybe we could have collected some lumps," Ross growled. "Got any more ideas?"

The doctor sipped his coffee. "No," he admitted. "I wonder—No, I don't suppose that means anything."

"That jingle? Sure it means something, Doc. It means I should have had my head examined for letting you talk me into that performance."

The doctor said rebelliously, "Maybe I'm wrong, Ross, but I don't see that you've had any ideas that panned out much better."

Ross got up. "All right," he admitted. "I'm sorry if I gave you a hard time. It's all this coffee and all the liquor underneath it; I swear, if I ever get back to a civilized planet I'm going on a solid diet for a month."

They headed for the room marked "Gents," Ross sullenly quiet, Doc thoughtfully quiet.

Doc said reflectively, " 'The price is ten cents.' Ross, could that mean a paper that we could buy on a newsstand, maybe?"

"Yeah," Ross said in irritation. "Look, Doc, don't give it another thought. There must be some way to straighten this thing out; I'll think of it. Let's just make believe that whole asinine radio program never happened." The attendant materialized and offered Ross a towel.

"Dime?" he said wearily.

Ross fished absently in his pocket. "The thing that bothers me, Doc," he said, "is that I know there are intelligent people somewhere around. I even know what they're doing, I bet. They're doing exactly what I tried to do: acted as stupid as anybody else, or stupider. I'd make a guess," he said, warming up, "that if we could just make a statistical analysis of the whole planet and find the absolute stupidest-seeming people of the lot, we'd——"

He ran out of breath all at once. His eyes bulged from the internal pressure of a thought too big for one mind to hold.

He looked at the men's-room attendant, and at the ten-cent piece in his own hand.

"You!" he breathed.

The attendant's face suddenly seemed to come to life. In a voice that was abruptly richer and deeper than before, the man said, "Yes. We wondered whether you would find us. We knew that if you deserved to, you would succeed."

14

They had a homeland, though perhaps it would be better to call it a rest camp. It was a gigantic island named Australia, and there they took Ross and Doc Jones. They flew in a car that sprouted no wings and flared no rockets, but raced through the thin ionosphere of half the world's girth, and held the setting sun suspended over the horizon all the way.

They lived there, invisible to the rest of the world. Often the goggling vacationers from the teeming cities of the great continents passed over in their rockets. (They weren't rockets. They were sluggish subsonic jets. But it made the children happy to think they had rockets, so pyrotechnic chemicals were added to the hot exhausts to make them sparkle.) Nothing could be seen from the "rockets" at forty thousand feet, and they never landed. They were not allowed to.

There on that island the guardians were born. There they spent their strange childhoods, learning such things as psychodynamics and teleportation. By the time they were eight months old or so they thought it amusing to chatter, with their toothless little mouths, of such things as Self and the Meaning of Meaning. By the age of eighteen months a dozen infants would join to chant the songs of Gödel and Wittgenstein in *terza rima*. But by the time they were two such childish pleasures were put behind them, with sighs of pleasant nostalgic regret. They would revert to them only for such purposes as love-making, or in their choral funeral addresses.

They were then of an age to begin their work: to learn, and to guard.

They were born on that island, and trained there for their terrible tasks. And at the end of their long lives they died there.

But in all the rest of their lives, from cradle to grave, they saw Australia only for short rest periods of a year or two, on leave from their grueling work. No one forced them to that work. No one possibly could. What made them consecrate their lives was conscience and compassion, and what they did was protect.

They were nursemaids.

When Ross grasped that point he was thunderstruck. "Nursemaids? You? You take *care* of all these people, all the millions of them?"

Their guide smiled gravely. "More than ten billion, actually," he said. "But yes. It is what we do. But we do not succeed," he added, stroking a musical instrument that he kept by his side. It had a dozen strings, but only one of them was played; its sound made Ross shiver.

"I don't understand," he said abjectly.

"No," the man agreed, "you do not. But the

reason you have come to Earth is that you have tried to. You deserve to know. Are you quite comfortable? Have you eaten enough? Do you need to rest?"

"We're fine," Ross said, glancing around. The room they were in had no walls, only gray shadows that baffled the eye as it looked for them. Obviously, he thought, these people were willing to be known only up to a point. Even to see what their places were really like was not permitted.

"Then," said the man, striking the string one more time and laying the instrument aside, "I will explain. I will start from the beginning.

"The pattern began to emerge clearly in the twentieth century. Priest-doctors of the time—they were called 'sociologists'—recognized the phenomenon even then. They did not understand what they saw, but they reported it well:

"The less educated people were outbreeding the more educated.

"The same was true almost everywhere. In the slums of the great industrialized cities, in the peasants' holdings of the hot countries, among the poor and ill-taught everywhere—if one walked through one of those neighborhoods one could think the whole world pregnant.

"Yet in a university town, or among the professional classes anywhere, one would see the impression wrong. These were prudent people. They saved. They planned. They postponed.

"A woman of that era had some three hundred and ninety opportunities to conceive a child. In the slums and the hills they took advantage of as many of them as they might. But around the universities, in the neighborhoods of the well-educated and the well-to-do, what was the score?

"First, education, until the age of twenty. This left two hundred and ninety-nine opportunities. Then, for perhaps five years, shared work; the car, the mortgage, the furniture, that two salaries would pay off earlier than one. Two hundred and thirty-four opportunities were left. Some of them were seized: a spate of childbearing perhaps would come next. But subtract a good ten years more at the end of the cycle, for the years when a child would be simply too late—too late for fashion, too late for companionship with the first-born. We started with three hundred and ninety opportunities. We have, perhaps, one hundred and forty-four left.

"Is that the roster complete? No. There is the battle of the budget: No, not right now, not until the summer place is paid for. And more. The visits from the mothers-in-law, the quarterly tax payments, the country-club liaisons and the furtive knives behind the brownstone fronts and what becomes of fertility—they have all been charted. But these are superfluous. The ratio 390:144 points out the inevitable. As three hundred and ninety outweighs one hundred and forty-four, so the genes of the child-rearers outweighed the genes of those who thought, and planned, and postponed.

"This was true for generations. For most of a century. And at the end of the century—it got worse.

"The educated and informed learned that children were a burden. Children hampered careers. Children cost more than yachts or summer homes on the sea. Even in the richest countries, pregnancy began to occur only in the most careless or improvident—teen-age girls provided most of the live births in the most advanced nations.

"The ratio grew worse.

"The average competence of the human race declined, and the careless billions, old enough to vote, chose leaders as much as possible like themselves. Children. Children of forty, or fifty, or seventy, but child-like in their disregard of consequence.

"And the children had terrible toys to play with, toys that could devastate a city or a nation, and—"

He paused to strike a note that sent the shadows quivering and made Ross's belly quake.

"And the toys went off. There was a war."

The man sighed and touched a square set in the floor beside him as he sat cross-legged. His gaze was in the shadows. With all the questions tearing at his throat, Ross dared not speak until a cart appeared from the shadows and rolled to a stop before them. The man took two small steaming handle-less cups from it and gave them to Ross and Doc Jones. The third cup he held in both hands under his bowed head, breathing the scented vapors for a moment before he swallowed.

Then he sat up, and his eyes focused on them again.

"After the war," he said, "the ratio continued to worsen, but then something else happened as well. The starships were built and went out to explore space. The best of the childlike ones went out in the ships, to explore, to colonize, to flee the playpen that Earth had become. When they went they chose others like themselves to join them, so that each ship was almost a family, bonded by kinship or by habits and tastes.

"We saw what was happening . . . and we fled.

"We did not seek another planet. We came here."

He stopped speaking and buried his face in the steam again.

Ross wrenched his eyes away from the guide at last. He cast a quick look at Doc Jones, rapt beside him; their eyes met and dropped. Ross took a long sip of the cooling beverage in his cup—scented, delicately fruity, wonderfully clarifying to the mind. He cleared his throat and ventured:

"But surely—you could do something! Travel to the stars—"

"No," said the man. "We cannot. We are prisoners of this planet."

"But you're the masters of it!"

"*Masters*? We are slaves! Nursemaids! We are fully alive only when we are among ourselves, here. We are as witless as they when we are with them, for how else could we be? For each of us there are square miles to stand guard over. We must keep our minds roving over the traps we dare not ignore, ready to leap out and straighten these children's toppling walls of building-blocks, ready to warn the child that sharp things cut and hot things burn. You have seen the blue lights that mark our intervention? Without them, can you imagine what catastrophes and agonies would come?"

"But— But— You're martyring yourselves for those idiots! Why not just let the accidents happen? Let them die?"

"Let—ten—billion—children—die? We are not such monsters." The man stared at Ross, deep eyes filled with anger and sorrow. Then he said:

"And we have failed, for if we have spared them untimely death, we have only given them a death in life instead.

"That is why you must help us now."

Ross strangled on a sip of the beverage. Beside

him, Doc Jones cried out in astonishment. "We?" Ross whispered.

"You," said the man, and now he smiled. It was a glorious smile that nearly masked the pain deep in his eyes. "All of you. For you are our problem, too, you and all your separate, sterile, dying planets.

"You see, the starfarers feared war, because they had seen what it did here. So they isolated each planet from the other with a wall of time. The nucleophoretic drive was kept secret from all but a few . . . and the few forgot, or didn't dare to use it.

"Crack those walls!

"Go back to your planets. Tell them of the F-T-L ships. Let your trader and builder make copies of the vessels, huge ones. Send trading expeditions out, to return in real time . . . and not always to return. Let some of the travelers stay. Let them bring back persons from the other worlds.

"Restore the missing genes. Pair Azor with Halsey's Planet. Cross the strains of the hundreds of worlds you have never seen. There is a term in genetics for what will happen: It is called 'hybrid vigor', and you will see a rebirth of humanity!"

The doctor said in a voice that crackled with excitement: "It could happen, Ross! It could do just what he says . . . but it will take time. Many, many years—"

"We have waited many, many years," said their guide. "We can wait more. But please begin! For when you have brought all the worlds together this one, too, will be a part of that new flowering. And we will be free!—free to become what is next for us."

Ross said faintly, "And what will you become?"

"You do not want to know what we will become," said the man gently. "Not yet." He gestured. The shadows began to recede. Blinking, Ross saw that they were in a large, warm room, and that they were not alone. A dozen or more of those others were sitting or standing around the walls, watching them. "Are you ready to begin?" he asked.

"Well— Sure, but— I mean, we need a ship—"

There were smiles on all the faces. "Oh, man," said their guide softly, "did you think we would let any of you leave when you were so close? Your ship was brought down here, and it is here still, not two miles away. Your friends are in it. And they are waiting for you."

"Ross!" Helena was hysterical with joy. Even Bernie was stammering and shaking his head delightedly, pumping their hands, hugging Doc. "Ross, dearest! We thought you had— And we felt so *bad* about leaving you— And the ship went all *funny*, and then it landed here, and these people brought us food and things but wouldn't talk— And I couldn't make it go up again—"

"It will go now," Ross promised. It did. They sealed ship. Ross took the controls. They rose gracefully to orbit and hung there, looking back on a blue-green planet with a single moon.

"We'll be back," said Ross. "But first we go to Halsey's Planet to start. Haarland will like his answer. It will mean he can build ships and prosper as a trader—and let others steal his designs and compete. We'll bridge the galaxy with F-T-L ships!"

Exultantly he set up the combination for Halsey's Planet on the board and threw in the drive, Helena standing proudly by his side. "And one other thing, dear Helena," he said. "A personal thing for the two of us. We'll be married as soon as we get to Halsey's Planet, if you'll have me."

"Oh, Ross," she breathed. "Is that what you want?"

"It's what I've wanted for quite a while," he said tenderly, and grinned. "Besides, it's our duty to the human race. And if you'll just sit down while Bernie makes us something to eat, I'll tell you why. . . ."

Joseph H. Delaney, co-author of *Valentina: Soul in Sapphire*, is back with his most ambitious work yet—a massive volume that is awesome in scope and stunning in execution.

The time is 18,000 years in the past. Aged and ailing, tribal shaman Kah-Sih-Omah has prepared himself to die, seeking final refuge far from the lands of his people. The time of his passing is near when alien beings chance upon him. As an experiment, they correct his body's "inefficiencies"—then depart, leaving behind something that could not be, but is.

Kah-Sih-Omah finds himself whole again, and accepts this as a gift from the gods. Accordingly, he returns to his people, overjoyed that he may once again protect and lead them. But he is met with fear and rejection, and must flee for his life. Soon he discovers the incredible abilities with which he has been endowed, and embarks on a centuries-long journey that takes him across much of Earth, as well as to other worlds. During his travels, he struggles with the question of why he was granted strange powers and an extended lifespan. The answer awaits him in the far future . . .

In the Face of My Enemy is a book rich in characterization and historical background, and one which is guaranteed to intrigue readers. A map tracing Kah-Sih-Omah's travels on Earth highlights this fascinating saga.

HAVE YOU FOUND YOURSELF ENJOYING A LOT OF BAEN BOOKS LATELY?

We at Baen Books like science fiction with real science in it and fantasy that reaches to the heart of the human soul—and we think a lot of you do, too. Why not let us know? We'll award $25 and a dozen Baen paperbacks of your choice to the reader who best tells us what he or she likes about Baen Books. We reserve the right to quote any or all of you...and we'll feature the best quote in an advertisement in <u>American Bookseller</u> and other magazines! Contest closes March 15, 1986. All letters should be addressed to Baen Books, 260 Fifth Avenue, New York, N.Y. 10001.

KILLER STATION

by Martin Caidin

A giant space station orbiting the Earth can be a scientific boon ... or a terrible sword of Damocles hanging over our heads. In Martin Caidin's *Killer Station*, one brief moment of sabotage transforms Station *Pleiades* into an instrument of death and destruction for millions of people. The massive space station is heading relentlessly toward Earth, and its point of impact is New York City, where it will strike with the impact of the Hiroshima Bomb. Station Commander Rush Cantrell must battle impossible odds to save his station and his crew, and put his life on the line that millions may live.

This high-tech tale of the near future is written in the tradition of Caidin's *Marooned* (which inspired the Soviet-American Apollo/Soyuz Project and became a film classic) and *Cyborg* (the basis for the hit TV series "The Six Million Dollar Man"). Barely fictional, *Killer Station* is an intensely *real* moment of the future, packed with excitement, human drama, and adventure.

Caidin's record for forecasting (and inspiring) developments in space is well-known. *Killer Station* provides another glimpse of what *may* happen with and to all of us in the next few years.

Available December 1985 from Baen Books
55996-6 • 384 pp. • $3.50

Terrorism is a fact of life in the modern world, and the United States is a prime target for terrorists. Our citizens have been attacked, kidnapped, and killed in Central America, Lebanon, and Iran, and many of these acts have been perpetrated by suicidal fantatics who will stop at nothing to accomplish their goals.

What if terrorists hit the ultimate target—Washington, D.C.? And what if they used the ultimate weapon—a nuclear bomb on a suicide run? In *The Forty-Minute War*, by Janet and Chris Morris, this is exactly what happens. Using a hijacked airliner, members of the Islamic Jihad detonate a nuclear bomb over the White House, and the President, absent at the time, initiates a nuclear exchange with the Soviets. In the aftermath, American foreign service officer Marc Beck finds himself on a mission to fly anticancer serum from Israel to the Houston White House. Beck deals with one cliffhanger after another during the desperate days that follow, as he falls into political intrigue and prepares to make the ultimate sacrifice to activate a top-secret project that is his country's only hope.

This surprising novel will shock you with its sudden, satisfying ending. The authors bring an intense level of realism to the story, combining it with drama and suspense to create a frightening, compelling novel that could be straight out of tomorrow's headlines. Janet Morris, who has been labeled one of the best storytellers we have by Jerry Pournelle, is well-known as co-author of *Active Measures*, the $10,000 prize novel. She is the author of several popular series, as well, including the four-book Silistra series from Baen Books, which has sold over a million copies worldwide.

Adventure, suspense, high-tech—*The Forty Minute War* has it all.